Going to Egypt

RED FOX DEFINITIONS

By the same author

IN THE MONEY

Going to Egypt

HELEN DUNMORE

RED FOX DEFINITIONS

A Red Fox Book

Published by Random House Children's Books
20 Vauxhall Bridge Road, London SW1V 2SA

A division of The Random House Group Ltd
London Melbourne Sydney Auckland
Johannesburg and agencies throughout the world

Copyright © Helen Dunmore 1992

1 3 5 7 9 10 8 6 4 2

First published in Great Britain by
Julia MacRae 1992

This Red Fox edition 2001

Printed and bound in Great Britain by
Bookmarque Ltd, Croydon, Surrey

Papers used by The Random House Group Ltd are natural, recyclable products made from
wood grown in sustainable forests. The manufacturing processes conform to the environmental
regulations of the country of origin.

THE RANDOM HOUSE GROUP Limited Reg. No. 954009

www.randomhouse.co.uk

ISBN 0 09 941195 4

For Ollie and Patrick

Chapter One

Going to Egypt. Going to Egypt, going to Corfu, ferry-hopping from island to island, travelling the Karakoram Highway. Eating ripe peaches off a tree or drinking Turkish coffee in a restaurant where it's still warm at midnight and there are kids running around the tables and fishing-boats down at the quay and someone playing a guitar. Or whatever they play in Turkish restaurants. I'll have to check that out. You've got to be accurate.

I'm a born traveller. I know I am. It's either in you, or it isn't. But at the moment I'm a born traveller who hasn't gone anywhere. If you leave out Birmingham and a trip to Scotland and a couple of days in Dublin with Dad. But just wait. I don't mean package deals, I mean real journeys, with maps and plans and all my stuff in one rucksack. I mean staying in places I like for a day or a week, then moving on. I mean talking to people. I mean going to all the countries that are opening up now the Berlin Wall's gone down. I mean people coming up and talking to me in Greek or Czech because I look as if I live there.

*

But at this moment I am on a train that's just sliding out of Paddington station. I'm sweaty and out-of-breath from tearing right across London on the hottest day we've had this August. I stand up to throw my rucksack into the luggage rack and the second I've got my back to him the fat man in the suit spreads out his thighs and takes over half my seat. But I know how to deal with that. He doesn't know he's messing with someone who's been going to school on the Tube for the past year. I don't say anything but I work out which corner of my sports bag has the Coke can in it and I let it swing as I sit down so that it rams hard into the tender flab just under his ribs. He can't help jumping and that's when I wedge myself in with the sports bag between us, and I sit back with a smile for the lady opposite. She smiles back at me. She's all right. She's got a Mills & Boon paperback and a paper bag of stripy mints on the tiny shelf which they've put there so your coffee can fall off it and spill all over you. She rustles the bag at me and says, "Like a mint, dear?" and I say, "Thanks a lot," and take one, and I just hope she isn't going to talk all the way, because I've got a lot to think about.

Mum will be half-way back across London by now. She didn't have time to see the train off, because she had to go to an emergency meeting at the Women's Refuge where she works. She does housing advice mainly, but it spills over into lots of other things, and there's always something going wrong, really awful things that I don't want to know about. The phone rings and she sighs and hauls herself up and then she goes on and on talking while first one lot of adverts comes on, then another. If she puts the phone down and comes straight back in it's usually

OK, but if she goes to the kitchen to put the kettle on I know what she's going to say even before she says it.

"Sorry, Colette, I've just *got* to go in. There's a problem. I'll have a quick coffee first. Have you finished your homework yet?"

And I tell her I finished it hours ago and I'll phone Angelina and ask her to come round for a bit while Mum's out.

My mum is thirty-seven. She had me when she was twenty-four, and when I was little we lived with my dad as well. I was seven when they split up. Mum kept our flat, and Dad moved right away to Birmingham. He didn't really want to, but he got a job there and it would have cost too much for him to get another flat in London, even round where we live. So I go to see him in Birmingham. I've been going on the train on my own since I was ten.

But this train, the train I'm on now, isn't going to Birmingham. It's got a name painted on it which I noticed when I got on, because it was so over-the-top. It's called THE BELLE OF CORNWALL. I suppose the idea is to make it sound so exciting that more people want to go on it, but have you ever seen anyone on a train who hasn't *got* to be on it? At this moment THE BELLE OF CORNWALL is sliding its way through joined-up nothing: industrial estates and supermarket depots and tower-blocks they've moved everybody out of. I'm tired after the rush across London to get to Paddington in time. If Mum hadn't been wearing her zig-zag jersey, I'd never have kept track of her on the concourse. People were milling around everywhere, falling over trolleys and losing little kids and dripping ketchup over their luggage from their FAST N' EEZY hot-dogs. Mum and I bashed our way through and bought me some sweets and stuff from the kiosk and then at last they

3

let us through onto the platform and Mum had to run. Mum looked really hot and tired. I told her in the morning not to wear that jersey because the forecast said it was going to be hot later, but she likes wearing it so much she put it on anyway. And it is lovely. She's going to make me one like it. You might wonder when my mum gets time to knit, with all the rushing about she does. She knits in meetings. She has to wash the jerseys out before she wears them for the first time though, because her knitting always smells of smoke. Everybody smokes at the meetings. Lots of women in the refuge smoke. Mum doesn't, but she says she would, if she'd been through what some of them have been through. So she puts up with it at meetings, even though she gets really horrible if people smoke in our flat. She goes round opening windows and taking away the ashtrays to clean them out every ten minutes. Dad smokes. Lots of the kids at our school smoke, but I don't tell her that.

The ticket-collector's coming. Of course I've got my ticket safe. Mum gave it to me. I put it in my sports bag inside zip-pocket . . . didn't I?

"Tickets please! ALL tickets please!"

He's coming nearer. Only four rows away. *Think*.

"Now, here are your tickets, Colette. Put the return right away, you won't need it till you come back."

My jacket pocket! The top one with the zip and the flap! I fumble it open and there's the ticket. The return ticket.

He's standing right over me now, taking the tickets of the fat businessman and the woman with the sweets. They've got theirs all ready. I stand up and feel in my jeans pocket. Nothing. He's waiting, smiling, tapping his punch-machine against his palm. I'm sweating and I know

4

my face has gone bright red. I dive into my jeans pockets again, hopelessly.

"I'm sorry," I gabble, "I can't find it but I know I've got it, look, I've got the return . . ."

The businessman smirks, pretending to read his paper. The woman opposite leans forward and says, "Have you tried your purse, dear?"

My purse! Of course! Why didn't I think of it? But *where is it?*

"Isn't that your purse behind you?" asks the ticket-collector.

I turn round and there down the side of the seat is the fat red edge of my purse. It must have fallen out of my sports bag when I whacked the businessman. And there in the purse is my beautiful British Rail ticket with the little word *out* written on it. Everybody is looking at me and smiling as the conductor puts my ticket into his machine and prints the date and time on it. I feel so embarrassed that I would welcome a train crash.

"Like another mint?" asks the woman, but this time I shake my head and look out of the window. Luckily my hair's long enough to make a curtain between me and the rest of the world when I need one. And I need one now. The businessman's taking over my seat again, inch by warm inch, as his thigh presses up against mine. And I haven't even got an umbrella. Angelina's brilliant with her telescope umbrella, in the Tube. Nobody messes with Angelina. So I take a deep breath and do the best I can with a bit of elbow work and coughing and looking around to make people notice what's happening.

And all at once there's a miracle: the woman with the sweets suddenly catches on and gives the businessman a really hard stare and says, "Excuse me, but I really do think this young girl needs a bit more room than you're giving her," in quite a loud voice.

And this time he shrinks up like a balloon someone's pricked. You'd never think he could fit into as small a space as he fits into now. And he turns red, like me, but dark and purplish, not bright. I'm not so keen on the 'young girl' bit, but all the same I give the woman a big smile, and a wink, at which she looks a bit surprised.

If only I was tall, like Angelina!

How many times have I said that? Hundreds, I expect. Angelina's the same age as me; well, a bit older, she's fourteen in December and I'm not fourteen till next May. But we're in the same class. We always have been, since we were five, and we went to the same playgroup before that. Angelina's mum and mine used to be quite good friends too, but they don't see so much of each other now Angelina's mum has got married again.

Angelina's tall, and she's strong. She does cross-country running on Sundays, but she says she's too heavy to make a real runner. She's not fat at all, but when I go to her runs I see what she means – some of the girls are so light they're almost scrawny, but they go like whippets.

Boys like Angelina, but they're a bit afraid of her. They say, "That Angelina!" She gets respect. I sometimes think that's the biggest difference between people: the ones who get respect, and the ones who don't. The trouble is, you never really know about yourself, which type of person you are. Or at least, I don't.

I didn't mean to go to sleep. The sun's pouring straight into my face now. It must have woken me up. I shift myself, all hot and sweaty and stiff and creased. The businessman's gone, and the woman with the sweets. Everyone's gone except for one boy with a Walkman in the bank of seats opposite, and he's asleep. The train's going really fast now, and outside there are small green fields, then some hills, low curving hills like the ones you draw when you're little. On the tables there are lots of messed-up newspapers, piles of drink cans and sandwich wrappers and plastic cups.

How long have I been asleep? I can't believe it. It's seven-thirty-four. That means I've been asleep for nearly two hours. And where are we? *Have I missed my stop?*

I lurch down the train and ask the first person I see, "Do you know where we are? Which was the last stop?"

He puts down his computer print-out and says, "Bristol."

What a relief. I know the stops because Mum's written them down for me. Weston's the next one. I go back to my seat and gather my stuff together. We're nearly there, and I haven't done any of the thinking I was going to do. As usual.

Chapter Two

I DON'T REALLY ENJOY the first few minutes of seeing Dad again. Perhaps some people might think that a girl who hasn't seen her father for three months would be longing to rush into his arms, and that there wouldn't be any problems, but in my experience it's not like that at all. For a start, I've usually grown a bit, and the way Dad reaches out to hug me doesn't quite match the size I am any more. His kisses bump on my nose, or he tries to pick me up then realises I'm too heavy as well as years too old. He seems to have to realise this every time. It's as if I go back to being seven in his mind, during the time he doesn't see me. Then we never know what to say. That's all right during the kissing and hugging bit, because all you have to do is say things like 'Oh Dad!' or 'It's great to see you, Colette!'

But then comes the difficult part, when everybody else is moving off the platform and we have to go too. I find myself making a fuss about things which don't matter at all, like me carrying my own case, just to fill up the silence. Or Dad says I must be hungry, let's get a meal, and I say

I'm not, because I know I couldn't eat anything yet, not the way I'm feeling.

So pretty often our first conversation is a bit like a quarrel. Let's face it, often it *is* a quarrel. Then, if things go well, we look at one another and laugh and it gets easier to talk. But if things don't go well, Dad gets a hurt, hot look round his eyes, though he never says anything, and I start getting too eager and telling him a whole pile of stuff about school and ice-skating and Angelina and why I haven't written more letters.

In fact, it can be awful. And the same goes for the other end, when I see Mum again and I'm still tight and miserable about leaving Dad and knowing I won't be seeing him again till a whole term's gone by. And a term's eternity. You can't even imagine the end of it, when you're just at the beginning.

But this time it's all right. It's not one of the awful times. I see Dad through the train window before he sees me, and that's the way I prefer it. He's standing under a hanging basket of flowers, with some of that trailing blue stuff nearly touching his head. He's tall, my dad. (*Why aren't I tall, like Dad?*) He's squinting against the evening sun, which is so bright that I shouldn't think he can see anything. Dad must have listened to the weather forecast first thing, because he's wearing a new light blue shirt, one I haven't seen, and his black drill Bermudas which used to embarrass me but have come into fashion now, so that's all right. He's suntanned. It doesn't take more than half an hour in a park in the middle of Birmingham to get my dad the sort of suntan people show off after two weeks in Corfu.

But in spite of being tall, and the shorts and the suntan and everything, he looks so tired and sad and eager all at once that I just want to put out my hand and blot out the sight of him standing there waiting for me.

The train slows and I jump out with my sports bag and rucksack, a bit sooner than I should have done while the train's still moving. And I stumble and go down on one knee and graze it, just a bit, but there's blood. So that's why this meeting is all right. Straight away we're right into the middle of how I can never wait for anything, and why does he always have to make such a fuss whenever I hurt myself.

And another good thing: this time I am hungry. Because I've been asleep in the train I haven't eaten the sandwiches I had with me, or the packets of Opal Fruits, or the apple or the banana, so I'm not feeling sick of food the way I usually do. And Dad fancies an Indian, and so do I because I've been out to the Rhogan Josh with Mum a couple of times now, for her birthday and my second-year exam treat, and I really like Indian food. I'm thinking of becoming a vegetarian. I would, if I could eat vegetable biryani and lassi and nan bread every day, but somehow I can't see Mum or me getting round to all that cooking.

And the next amazing and good thing is that Dad has got a car. We walk out of the station as if we're going to get a taxi or a bus, and he doesn't say one word, just keeps on steering me past the queues and across to the car-park. And then he stops. It's a little red Renault, quite new and not a single bash in it.

"Dad! Is it yours? It's brilliant!"

Well, it's not really Dad's, but he's got the use of it this week, because Clive is using the van. Clive is Dad's partner. They do fitted kitchens, for people who want their cupboards and things hand-carpentered. I've seen some of the jobs he's done. The kitchens look beautiful, because

Dad and Clive work with natural woods and lots of different stains, in whatever colours the clients want. The surfaces have that silky feel wood has when it's been planed and sanded down and polished. And the units are solid wood all through. You don't open the cupboards and find chipboard crumbling away inside.

But the kitchens are very, very expensive. It's taken a long time for Dad and Clive to build up enough clients, because it's all word-of-mouth and recommendations, but Dad says things are really starting to happen now.

Dad wasn't always a carpenter. He used to be a teacher when I was little, teaching primary school kids; then about four years ago he retrained. I think he's happy doing the fitted kitchens. Or fairly happy. Happier than when he was teaching.

Dad's made stuff for my bedroom. A desk, a bedside table and chest combined, and my bedstead. He brought it all up to London in his van one Saturday about a year ago. Mum didn't say anything beforehand. She just said, "It's about time we had a clear-out of your room, Colette," at which I screamed a bit and said how much I loved all the old stuff and how I'd always had it 'ever since you and Dad were together' (*I go red now, thinking of what I said*).

But Mum took no notice, which was as well, and for a few days I really liked my empty echoey room which suddenly looked big and light like a room by the seaside. And then Dad rolled up with the stuff. When I went to sleep that night my room smelled of new wood. I felt like Heidi in her attic up in the mountains. I used to love that story when I was a kid.

"It'll be fantastic having the car for the holiday, Dad."

He looks pleased, and when we've both got in and we've slung my bags in the back he says, "Have a look in the glove compartment. I've been to the tourist places and got all these maps and brochures. I thought with the car, we could go all over. You know, really get to know the place."

I flip through the wodge of paperwork. From the look of it, we've come to the most exciting, sunny, historical, friendly, clean and family-loving part of the British Isles. Why does anybody bother to go abroad?

I look out of the window.

"I'll take you along the sea-front," Dad says as he clashes the gears and we shoot off in fourth. He stalls, swears a bit and then calms down.

"I'm not used to this car yet," he explains, unnecessarily.

There are crowds of people on the sea-front, mainly old grannies and grandads, and lots of girls of about sixteen with very high heels and white stilettoes, all linking arms and managing to eat burgers at the same time. Smells of food blow in through the car windows. Burgers, fish and chips, vinegar, fresh hot doughnuts, candy-floss, popcorn. There are hot-dog stands on the promenade, and all the cafés are open, belting out music.

We park not far from the Indian restaurant, and Dad waves at the sea. "Look! The tide's in."

I glance at the water, surprised. After all it's not so very amazing, is it? The tide's always coming in or out, at the seaside. Dad laughs.

"It's a bit of a rarity here," he says. "You have to make the most of it. I've got a tide-table."

The sea is quite an interesting colour, as long as you don't start thinking it ought to be blue. It's grey, and brown, a light metallic colour, with glossy patterns on it from the sun, which is going down fast now. There are lots of people down at the water's edge, shrieking and hopping about in the brown foam. It's funny how you can't look at people paddling in the sea without wanting to rush down yourself.

"Do you want to go and have a look at it?" Dad asks.

But I shake my head. I'm starving, and the front of the restaurant looks nice, with big crimson letters on a blue background, saying GANGES. I can't wait.

For the next hour all we say to each other is

"What's brinjal?"

"How many parathis can you eat?"

"Wow! This lime pickle's hot!

"I'll swap you an onion bhaji for your poppadum."

"Is there any more chutney?"

"You can fish out my prawns as well if you want them."

"What sort of ice-cream is kulfi?"

"Sweets with coffee?"

"Yes, please!"

But when I see the bill I go quiet. Dad pays it, smiling and telling the man how much we've enjoyed the meal, and we go out of the restaurant on a wave of good feelings, but I'm really worried.

"Dad."

"Mm?"

We're nearly at the car. I slow down and mumble, "Dad. Listen. While we're on holiday, I don't want you to think you've got to spend a load of money on me all the time."

For a minute Dad looks really angry. Or maybe it's

something else, not anger exactly. Then he says, "Listen, Colette. Let's for once forget about being careful. This is our holiday money. It's not meant for something else. I'm not going to pay the bills with it, and I haven't taken it out of your mother's maintenance. It's *holiday* money. When it's gone, it's gone. Have you got that?"

But he looks all right again, and not angry with me, so I just say, "Yes boss," and dodge round to the passenger door.

When Dad first left, when I was about seven, he had a bed-sit about half-a-mile away for the first few months, before he went to Birmingham. It was a horrible bed-sit really, and I never wanted to go there because there was a strange man downstairs who shouted and banged on the ceiling. I wouldn't mind him now, but I did then. So Dad used to take me out all the time when I went to see him, and one Saturday after we'd been to the Tower in the morning and McDonald's for lunch and a puppet theatre in the afternoon because it was raining, plus all the Tube fares, I went rushing in to Mum the minute we got back to the flat, and told her everything we'd been doing. She really hit the roof and shouted at Dad. I can still remember some of the things she said, about *'buying Colette's love,'* and *'bribing your own daughter with junk'* and *'if it's going to be like this, I'm going to go back to court'*. Then I went into my bedroom and hid behind the door so I wouldn't hear any more.

And it was all so stupid, because Dad was just desperate. He couldn't think what else to do with me, on a rainy Saturday in London when you can't say, "I've had enough of this. Let's go home and have a cup of tea and watch television."

We get in the car, and drive off. It's one of those dusky

warm August evenings when you feel you could stay up all night. We can hear music spilling out of the sea-front discos as we drive along. We drive up a steep hill, then swing round into a little narrow road between dark trees.

"This is the toll road," says Dad. "And that's the sea, down below you."

I crane down through the window and I see the shine of water through the trees. It's nearly dark now. Far out, a lighthouse flashes, once, twice.

"We're nearly home," Dad says.

That's something about Dad: no matter how short a time he's living anywhere, he always calls it home.

Chapter Three

IT'S MORNING. I got through the night. I must have done, because the sun's falling on my face through the gap in the curtains. I blink and dive down the side of the bed to find my watch. I never wear it in bed, because I dream a lot and I flail around and get my watch caught in my hair. And that gives me more dreams, ones that seem to go on for hours instead of the few seconds it takes me to wake up. But I won't go into that now. The sun's shining, and the chalet is absolutely quiet.

I have never slept in such a noisy place in my life. I felt as if I was inside a matchbox and somebody was striking matches on the walls. I was really tired, after the journey and meeting Dad again and unpacking and Dad showing me where everything was. Then I had to wash standing on one leg with the big T-shirt I wear in bed clenched between my teeth so it wouldn't get wet. The shower leaks, and there's mould round the tiles. The wash-basin is the size of a basin on a cross-channel ferry. I didn't expect the water to be hot, but it was, because Dad had left the immersion on for hours by mistake. Luckily it's not the kind that overheats and blows up. I didn't wash my hair, though, because although the water in the shower was hot, there wasn't much of it.

This is a holiday chalet, that's why it's so noisy and everything is either not quite the right size or much lighter than you think it's going to be. There's a living-room, with a sofa-bed. That's where Dad sleeps. There's one bedroom. The woman who lets it came round yesterday and Dad said she was quite surprised there were only going to be two of us in the chalet.

"Seems a waste, really," she said, "when the chalet sleeps four easily – and we've had five or six, sometimes. Your daughter could have brought a friend down."

I'd like to see this chalet with five or six people sleeping in it. And even better, five or six people trying to get washed and dressed and have breakfast. There's a picnic table in the kitchen, which is fine for Dad and me, and I suppose the other four could eat in the garden, as long as it wasn't raining. There'd be the toast burning because nobody could get round the others to switch off the toaster (it doesn't pop up on its own – we tried), and all the time you were eating you'd hear the toilet flushing through the wall, over and over because it takes about ten minutes for the tank to fill up each time.

Last night I heard Dad moving around for hours. I heard him pull back the ring-tab on each can of Guinness: one, then another, then another. He smoked a lot. I could smell it under the door. There's a portable TV and he had it on very low, just too low for me to hear the words. He had quite a battle with the sofa-bed. At first he couldn't open it out at all. He was grunting and pulling and thumping, then I heard a can skitter off across the floor. Empty, by the sound. Then there was a flump and he'd done it but I think he must have caught his finger or something, because I heard some quite loud swearing for a few minutes, and it sounded as if he was hopping about a bit and banging into more things. In fact that was when I fell asleep. I'd given up on the idea that I was ever going to get any peace and quiet.

The curtains are very thin striped ones, made of that Indian cotton which was in fashion when Mum and Dad were young. We've got some awful photos of Mum in a full-length striped dress made out of it, with her hair down to her waist, standing under trees in a wood somewhere, gazing into the distance, miles from anywhere and anyone . . . But of course she can't have been, considering that there was someone with a camera about six feet away. Mum can't stand photos of her when she was young. She was going to take them out of the album, but I wouldn't let her.

"Don't we all look *young*!" she says.

Well, of course they do. After all they were young, weren't they? Well, youngish.

"No, you don't understand what I mean. It's just that at the time, you don't realise how young you really are. But now, I *feel* quite young but when I look in a mirror, I see I'm not."

I cheer her up by telling her she's only thirty-seven, and that two of my friends' mothers had babies when they were forty-one. She throws a cushion at me, but it misses.

I've told you all the bad things about the chalet. Now here are the good ones:

It doesn't feel as if you're in a house at all. It's more like being in a tent with thin wooden walls. And I love camping.

You couldn't do much housework if you tried. There's

a little soft broom for sweeping sand out of the kitchen door, and some bathroom cleaner, and that's about it.

It's so light. You can't see the sea, because there's a high bank of grass at the end of the garden, but from there you step up onto the sea-wall. The chalet's below sea-level, and Dad says that he saw some dried seaweed on the grass.

The air smells quite different from London air. Last night we stood in the garden in the dark. I could smell the sea, and damp grass and horses in the paddock next to the chalets, instead of petrol fumes and take-aways and dog-dirt on the pavements. Don't get me wrong, I love Finsbury Park, at least I think I do. I've always lived there, so I don't know anywhere else. But it's still good to smell trees and horses and see stars because there aren't any streetlights in the way.

I kick off the duvet and get out of bed. There's a bubbly striped rug by the bed, but no carpet, just plain boards. They feel cool and smooth. My room opens off the kitchen, and the living-room is the other side. I open the door, and peer in. It's very dark, because Dad has hung a blanket over the curtains. He hates waking up early. Dad is humped up on the sofa-bed, with a bit of his hair and his ears sticking out of the top of his sleeping bag. He hasn't bothered with the sheets and quilt Edna Tench left out for him. That's really her name. The room still smells of smoke. Dad grunts, so I close the door gently. I creep off to the bathroom. The toilet flushes with a groan like an empty stomach, but I don't think it'll wake Dad yet.

In spite of the Indian meal, I am starving again. I look out on the doorstep without much hope. To my amazement there are two bottles of milk there, one Jersey and one semi-skimmed, and a packet of fruit yoghurts. Dad will have got the Jersey milk for me, because he thinks I'm too skinny. The doorstep isn't really a doorstep. There is a little flight of wooden steps leading down the side of the chalet from the kitchen door. The sun is pouring onto the top step, and I decide that's where I'll sit to eat my breakfast. I'm encouraged by the milk, and I look through the cupboards quite hopefully. Dad has done amazingly well! There's a huge box of Rice Krispies, which used to be my favourite cereal. I suppose Dad thinks it still is. There's a sliced loaf, and six eggs, and some raisin muffins, and six bananas. In the tiny fridge I find some sunflower margarine and a carton of orange juice, plus more milk. I wonder if Dad is on a health kick now, like Mum. Mum is practically a vegan. Then I spot a packet of streaky bacon in the back of the fridge. Dad's favourite – bacon sandwiches for breakfast with HP sauce, and thin slices of fresh tomato. That's a relief. I don't want him to change too much.

I split and butter two raisin muffins, pour myself some orange juice, and put the kettle on. With the back door open I can hear all the birds. I know one of them, because it's a wood pigeon and we have those in London. The sun is very bright, and the blue and white striped mugs glitter on their hooks by the sink. It's great being up on my own, with no need to worry about the time, and Dad asleep in the next room. I don't need to worry about him, as long as he's asleep. When he's awake I have to keep on checking him, even though I know it's stupid. Is he happy, or is he fed up? Is he really smiling or just pretending to smile? Am I doing the right thing?

I can't remember if it used to be like this when Dad lived at home.

The sun on the back step feels really hot, even though it's only eight-thirty. When I've made my tea, I bring it back out so I can sunbathe. I stretch out my arms. I want to get a proper tan this week, so I've got my pink sleeveless T-shirt on, and shorts. I wish I had someone here who could do my hair in a French plait for me.

As I finish the raisin muffins, there's a movement in the corner of the paddock. Two boys are opening the gate. They're not wearing riding-clothes. They haven't even got hard hats. Both of them are wearing jeans and black T-shirts. They look quite different though, even wearing the same clothes. One of them is much taller and he has dark shiny hair. I can't see his face at first, then he turns round and starts to talk to the horse. He's got a dark, thin face, very tanned. He doesn't see me. The horse puts her nose down into his hand, and he rubs her side. The other boy hangs back a bit. I wonder how old they are? They're definitely older than me. The taller one could be sixteen or seventeen. The other one, the sandy-haired one, looks about fourteen. Maybe fifteen. Yes, he looks like a third-year. The taller one looks as if he's left school. They start putting stuff round the horses' necks. I've never been riding so I don't know what it's all called, but I can see they aren't putting saddles on the horses. They must be good riders. They don't talk much to each other. They're too far away for me to hear what they say, but I can hear their voices.

The taller boy leads out the dark-brown horse, and the other leads out the black-and-white one. The horses look a bit rough, not beautifully groomed like the horses you see on TV. I wonder if the horses belong to the boys, because they seem to know them so well. Or perhaps they work here. The younger boy could be doing a holiday job.

They still haven't seen me, and I don't really want them to. I always wish I knew people already, because I really hate talking to them for the first time. Besides, I'm afraid that if they see me at this distance, they'll just think I'm a kid. It's being small again, and a bit skinny, and not having big boobs, and not wearing make-up most of the time. Angelina doesn't, either. Wear make-up much, I mean. She gets pissed off because the big chains hardly sell any make-up for black girls. She can get it at the chemist near us, but what she wants is just to go into Boots and try millions of different colours from all the ranges. You don't get much choice at our local chemist. But Angelina's definitely got big boobs. When we go swimming, boys keep glancing down while they try to chat her up. This pisses her off too.

"I can tell you're really interested in me as a person," she says. Only Angelina can say things like that, at the time, not later like I often do when I suddenly think of what would have been a brilliant thing to say in a particular situation.

The boys lead the horses across the field, out of the gate and down the lane and then I can't see them any more. There are some small sharp-edged clouds coming up over the hill, and it's not quite as warm now. I get up and wander down the steps and round the side of the chalet. The garden is quite long, scrubby and sandy, with some tough-looking bushes and two clumps of red-hot pokers, one at each side of the gate. I go through the gate, across the small empty road and climb the steps onto the top of the sea-wall.

The bay is full of water. Sand comes right up to the top of the sea-wall. In fact it isn't really a wall on this side, the beach side. The sand's very coarse and pebbly, and there are tufts of grass growing out of it, which look as if they'd cut your hands if you touched them. There's quite a lot of rubbish, too: crisp packets and King Cone wrappers and polystyrene burger packs. Farther down, where the sand slopes to the water, there's a thick line of seaweed and driftwood and more rubbish, all matted up together. The bay looks just like a bowl someone's filled up, from the woods at one side past the long flat stretch of sand to the headland. I kick off my trainers and walk down the rough sand, into the water.

Chapter Four

I WADE OUT VERY slowly, trying not to disturb the surface of the water. It's much warmer than I'd expected, and I can't see the bottom, even though the water's only a bit past my knees. When you bend down and look closely, you can see millions of particles of sand or mud, hanging there in the water, but when you straighten up again, it just looks like dirty water. I stop wading and stand still. I can hear birds singing in the woods by the water. It doesn't sound right. When we go to Brighton, there aren't any birds except seagulls, going round in circles then dive-bombing for bits of hot-dog and looking at you with their evil eyes. But I can only see one gull here, a fat silent one rocking away on the water, much farther out, doing nothing.

Suddenly I step down. The water goes right up my thighs, and my left foot sinks in sludgy soft mud. I nearly fall over, but then I pull my foot out and step back and up. I must have been on a sandbank. I rub my foot hard against the sand to get rid of the sucking, oozy feeling of the mud, but when I stand on one leg and look, I'm still smeared with black mud, between my toes and inside my ankle and up the back of my leg. This must be the mud Dad warned me about: the famous Weston mud, he called it.

"It's not dangerous here, but you have to be careful on the main beach, by the mouth of the Axe."

I shiver. I have a nightmare about being caught by my feet, with something coming after me so I'm trying to run, but I just can't lift my feet though my heart's pounding and I'm sobbing with effort and the thing's getting nearer and nearer . . . And then I wake up.

Or at least, that's when I've always woken up so far.

After this, I've had enough of paddling. I'm wading back to the beach, which is much farther away than I'd realised, about two hundred yards, when I see the two boys riding their horses down the beach – straight down the beach and into the water. The horses don't hesitate at all when they get to the water's edge. They seem to love it. They splash through the shallow water with their heads up, looking pleased with themselves. They are going to pass quite close to me. Suddenly I feel a bit stupid, paddling on my own, way out here, but there's not much else I can pretend to be doing. I haven't even got a fishing net. It's no good. They are bound to think I'm about eleven, on a nice seaside holiday with my mummy and daddy. So I just shade my eyes against the sun on the water, and watch the boys on their horses. The sandy fair one smiles as they go by, and slaps his horse's side when the horse seems inclined to stop and take a look at me.

"GET on, you great nosy thing!" he says, and the horse shakes its head and gets on. The boy smiles again as they go by. His face is all freckly close-to, with light eyes screwed up against the sun.

The dark one doesn't look at me. He's bored, unsmiling.

They go out much farther than I've been, then suddenly the horses are swimming. The boys must be soaked through, but they don't care, they keep the horses' heads pointed towards Wales. The dark boy leans right forward, with his arms round the horse's head, as if he's whispering to her. She turns, and swims in my direction. I see both their faces: the horse's long muzzle, with wide nostrils and shiny staring eyes, and the boy's face. I thought his eyes would be dark, but they're not. They're yellowish. I suppose you would call it hazel. I stand still with the water lapping round my thighs, staring at them both. It seems ridiculous to say hello to someone on a swimming horse, out in the middle of the sea. About fifty yards from me, the horse finds its feet. For a minute it stumbles and quivers, then it makes a scrambling, climbing movement and hoists itself up onto the sandbank. The water streams round its sides. Then the two horses neigh to each other, like people calling across the baths when they're having a swim. The other horse is still far out, swimming. It looks brilliant. I wish I could do it. The dark boy splashes past, leading his horse up to the beach. He doesn't say anything, but he looks sideways at me and smiles, a creased-up, Red Indian sort of smile that flicks on for about half a second, then flicks off again so that I'm not sure if I really saw it or not. It's so quick that I don't have time to smile back.

I tell Dad about the horses later on, when we're having breakfast: my second, his first. Sure enough out come the bacon and tomato and HP sauce sandwiches. I have some toast, and a few Rice Krispies, just to keep him company, and we make another pot of tea. But all too soon Dad has got out the brochures and the map and he's pushed the plates aside so that he can spread the whole lot out on the kitchen table. Words like 'Let's just relax' or 'Why not leave the washing-up till later?' mean nothing to Dad when he's in this mood. We are going to do Weston, and the Mendips, and Cheddar, and the whole of Somerset and a good part of the surrounding counties, too. And did I realise that was Wales, just across the water? My heart sinks.

I don't want to go to places like that. I want to travel. My aim in life is to be a foreign correspondent on a London paper. I don't see myself as a TV journalist, because I have the feeling I'm always going to be a bit too small. My head will only come half-way up the screen when I'm standing against a background of bombed buildings or refugees. People won't take me seriously. Kate Adie is one of my heroines. She's so tough and cool and she won't take any crap from anybody. She doesn't freak out when rocket-shells start falling around her, and she doesn't make a big deal out of it either. She keeps on talking in her normal voice, as if she actually wants to tell you something, instead of trying to impress you with what a macho person she is to be in a place where there are real guns going off and real people getting killed.

I'm not stupid. I know it takes years to get anywhere like that. I'm planning to do a journalism and new technology course when I leave school. I've found one where you study French and German too, and spend a year in Europe. Then I'll go anywhere.

This year our school's running a Travel-Writing award. It's based on a newspaper award that's been running for years. Of course it's not so high-powered, but the prize is brilliant. It's been donated by a local firm which is a branch of a multi-national corporation, and it's a week-long trip to Amsterdam, where the corporation has its headquarters. You stay with a family which has teenage kids. For three of the days you go to high school there, and the idea is that you gather material for an article about the Dutch school system – our local paper's said it'll publish the article, but I'd try the *Young Guardian* page too. You could write a really good article, if you interviewed lots of the kids about what it's *really* like there. There's a big Green movement in Holland, way ahead of ours. I'd write about that, too.

I've wanted to visit the Anne Frank house ever since I read her diary when I was eleven. I want to look out of the windows she looked out of, and see the film star pictures she pasted on the walls when she was in hiding. I try to imagine what it must have been like for her to live up there, whispering and not flushing the toilet and never singing in the daytime, day after day, for years, while the people in the offices downstairs were just carrying on working as normal. But I can't imagine it.

You know when something bad happens to you, something really bad though not as bad as what happened to Anne Frank, you can't believe that everything else just keeps on going. Your friends still muck about in class and talk about whether they're going out tonight or not, even if you're feeling the world's ended. Every so often they remember and look at you to see if you're still sad, and they're really relieved if you're not. It happened to me when my dad went away, though of course we were all really little then, and what my friends were talking about was how Joanna had had her ears pierced, the first one of us to get it done, and whose Mum was going to let *her* have it done as well. I remember staring and staring at Joanna's studs – they were gold, with garnets.

Why can't I keep my mind on one thing? Why does it keep skittering off the subject? I knew I ought to have done all this thinking when I was on the train.

I might as well forget about the travel-writing prize. There are lots of kids in our school who don't go anywhere much for their holidays, but there are plenty of others who go abroad, to Spain or Corfu or even to Florida. Alex Riley's going to Mexico, if you can believe it. He had to have millions of injections before he went. And there's a girl I don't know very well, in the fourth year, whose parents are taking her to Egypt. Egypt! Well really. Unfortunately she happens to be brilliant at English as well, so I expect she'll be scribbling away about the pyramids and the camels and how sorry she feels for all the beggars. Feeling sorry for beggars is a good move for a travel writer. It shows you aren't a heartless Western tourist. You're a real traveller. It's even better if you make friends with lots of people who live in tiny villages and don't speak a word of English, and keep giving you things to eat even though they've hardly got anything for themselves.

I doubt if I'll find many people like that in Weston-super-Mare.

Back to reality. Dad's still poring over the brochures. To my horror he's marking out what look like very long walks over hills. That's the trouble with adults who live in cities. Once they get out of them, they go completely mad and start wanting to walk ten miles a day across fields full of nettles and enormous cows that look like bulls, and they keep stopping to look at wild flowers which they say are protected by law so nobody can pick them. Even if there are hundreds. Mum's exactly the same, when we go camping. Always looking for mushrooms and blackberries at the wrong time of year.

In fact, when I think of all the ways in which Dad and Mum are exactly the same, I really wonder why they ever got divorced. It isn't even as if they've found anybody else. Mum had a boyfriend for about a year, but it didn't work out. He was called Steve, and he used to take us out in his car on Sundays. I quite liked him. He was a bit creepy with me at first, but he got more normal after a couple of months. I never said anything to Dad about Steve. I don't really want to know whether Dad's got any Steves of his own tucked away in Birmingham either. I don't mean Steves, I mean Stephanies. Really awful Stephanies with red pencil skirts and tans and 9-carat gold jewellery.

"This is good potholing country, too," says Dad enthusiastically.

"People come from all over the country to go caving in the Mendips. We'll go up there, shall we?"

"All right, Dad," I say faintly.

Potholing! I can't think of anything worse. I even have to do deep breathing in the Tube sometimes, when the train stops in the middle of the tunnel and everybody looks round and nobody says anything. I don't mind mountains. I wouldn't even mind falling off a mountain, if you know what I mean. You know how you try to think about which ways you wouldn't mind dying, even though you don't really want to die in any of them. I like being high up. I don't mind the edges of cliffs, either. I really freaked Mum out once, on Beachy Head.

But imagine being trapped underground, in a narrow

tunnel with no light, and the noise of water dripping, and the feeling that the air's going to run out and you can't move.

"Roight!" says Dad, pretending to be Somerset. "We'll go up and have a look at these here Mendips today, then. I'll clear this lot, you get started on the picnic."

Chapter Five

"WELL, THAT WAS great, wasn't it?" Dad asks. I nod. I can't say anything because I'm swallowing a mouthful of cold, yellow delicious shandy. We're in a pub garden a few miles from Priddy, where the potholes are.

"I quite fancy having a go at it myself," says Dad thoughtfully.

"As long as you don't expect me to go with you," I answer warningly, as I scoop up another forkful of thick-cut chips out of my chicken-in-a-basket.

It's great eating in pubs. We don't have to think of shopping, or cooking once we get home. Mum being practically a vegan means that there's always a mound of vegetables on our sink, ready to be peeled. Great big knobbly things, with dirt all over them. That's because they're organic. Mum gets them from a wholefood co-op down the road, where everybody's so laid-back you end up serving yourself, and telling them what things cost. Maybe one day I'll put the money in the till myself and take out the change.

"You can have the rest of my chips if you like," says

Dad, pushing them over. He's trying to fatten me up again. I spear his biggest chip and douse it in the puddle of vinegar at the side of my plate.

Dad's drinking Guinness as usual. I remember when I used to poke my finger in his glass and skim off some of the head and then lick my fingers. I still like the taste, though Guinness is too heavy for me. I can't imagine Dad drinking anything else. He doesn't like ordinary beer. The only other drink he has is a whisky in the evenings, just before he goes to bed. I can't stand the smell of whisky. It turns my mouth inside out, the way it goes just before you're sick.

"D'you think they're still down there?" I ask.

"They're probably underneath us right now," says Dad, and I can't help looking down.

We were just walking across a field of long grass and wild flowers when we saw these three men coming down the path. They were wearing lots of gear, and they had ropes, and bright yellow helmets with lights in them. They didn't say anything to us. We watched them climb over the stile into the next field, where there was a clump of trees. Then they stopped, and after a lot of unloading the gear and getting themselves sorted out, they disappeared. One moment they were standing in the sunshine, in the middle of an ordinary field, the next they were gone. We went to have a look. There was a wet narrow hole, just under the trees. You could look down it a little way, then it went on and on in darkness. I called down it, not very loudly because I didn't want the potholers to hear me, and there was an echo, a horrible one, dull and short and spiteful.

I shiver, thinking about it, even though the sun's still

quite warm. Suddenly I feel terribly tired, so tired I don't even want to lift my glass and drink the rest of the shandy.

"How about a walk along the promenade when we get back?" says Dad brightly. "Or we could see what's on at the cinema."

"Yeah," I say. I feel a thousand miles away from him. I feel as if *I'm* underground, sealed off from everybody by layers of cold rock and dripping water.

All at once I long to be with Angelina and Si and Matt and Josine. There's an open-air swimming pool about a mile away from where we live. All the kids from our school go there in the holidays. You can buy a season ticket for £8 if you're under sixteen, and then you can go as much as you want and stay all day. It's really nice there. The water always looks blue, even when it's cloudy, because there are blue tiles round the edge of the pool. I love the smell when you come in through the turnstiles. It's a mixture of chlorine and suntan oil and cut grass, and I'd recognise it anywhere with my eyes shut. The changing-rooms are underground, and there are portholes cut into the side of the pool so you can see all these wavy legs swimming by. Sometimes people swim underwater down to the portholes and look through them, and you can see their faces, all moony because the glass distorts them, with their hair going straight up, if they've got long hair.

There's grass all round the pool, and a couple of big old trees at the end, back by the wall so the leaves don't drop in the water. We usually sit up on the top terrace. There are concrete steps all the way up, and people lie on them sunbathing, then just roll off down into the water. There's a café, but it only sells drinks and crisps and stuff, so one of us goes out to the Indian takeaway and gets onion bhajis and samosas. We stay till about six o'clock, then lots of us walk back together, and we go on to someone's house for the evening. Mum usually gives me money for a takeaway in the holidays, because with her work you never really know what time she'll be home. I ring her and tell her whose house I'm at. We don't go out much in the evenings, except to the youth club. You get fights at the discos, really bad ones, and besides it's too expensive. This year I've been doing a free newspaper round with Angelina. We get £12.00 a week which isn't much when you split it two ways, but it helps.

I don't tell Mum everything about what I do when I'm out with my friends, but I tell her some of it. She knows most of my friends, anyway, because they come round to our flat quite a lot. She's known Si all his life; he's always lived round here and when we were little we went to the same childminder one day a week. And as I said before, I've always known Angelina.

But with Dad, I can't talk about my friends. There's no point. He doesn't know any of them, except perhaps he remembers Angelina a bit, and he doesn't seem to realise how old we are.

This is Dad: What've you been up to so far these holidays, love?

Me: Oh you know, nothing much. Just mucking about with my friends.

Dad: I expect you and Mum get out and about a lot, don't you? I read in the papers there was a fantastic new space exhibition at the Science Museum.

Me: She's *working*, Dad!

Dad: Doesn't she take time off? She must do! In the school holidays?

Me: (*gabbling again, not wanting Dad to think that Mum's neglecting me, terrified he's going to get on to Mum about What's Happening To Colette During the Summer Holidays. Phone calls, angry letters, Mum shouting, Mum going on at me, Mum crying . . .*) Oh yes of course, yeah, we have a brilliant time, Mum took me to the zoo last week, she loves the holidays because we can do stuff together . . . (*Help! I'm going right over the top here. The zoo – I ask you.*)

Dad: I wish I lived nearer to London.

At this point I have a terrible picture of myself spending the entire summer going to the History Museum or the Science Museum on alternate days, with Dad or Mum. Has Dad got the faintest idea what Tube fares are like these days? The Science Museum is in *Kensington* for heaven's sake.

Me: Yes, I wish you lived nearer, too.

I often wonder if everybody spends as much of their time lying to their parents as I do. I don't feel too bad about lying to Mum. Anyway she spots it most times: like when Jade's parents went away and Jade had a party, and I told Mum I was spending the night at Angelina's. Mum didn't say anything to me, but she must have been on the phone to Angelina's mother like a flash, because by the time I got back from school that day she had got the whole story. She'd even found out about Jade's party. She stopped me going. In the end I was quite glad about that, though of course I didn't tell Mum. Jade had only asked about twenty kids, but some of them must have talked about it and lots of much older boys turned up and tried to get in. Jade was really frightened, but luckily the neighbours knew her mum and dad. They've got three sons, in their twenties but they still live at home, all really big, and all into weight-training and body-building. They soon got rid of the boys. They made everybody go home, and they made Jade and Alex and Si and Ranjit clean the whole place up so it looked immaculate. Jade's mum was really pleased when she got back. At least, she was until the neighbours told her what had happened.

So Mum does tend to check up on me these days. There's a particular way she says, "Don't lie, Colette," very matter-of-fact, when I tell her I haven't got any home-work tonight so can I go ice-skating, or that we're not really having exams this year, just sort of tests.

I'm on holiday by the seaside. The sun is shining, and I've just had a lovely day out with my dad. He's bought me a meal in a pub. We might go to the cinema later. He smiles at me over his glass of Guinness and says,

"Cheers, love. Happy holidays!" and I smile back.

So why aren't I happy? Why do I feel like saying something that will kill Dad's smile? Why do I long to be somewhere else, though I don't know where? Why does the way Dad smiles at me make me want to cry?

His hair's thinning a bit on top. I'm not the only one changing, getting older. I've never wished this before, but perhaps, after all, I do wish he had a Stephanie of his own, even if she did have stiletto heels and a white hand-bag. Someone who'd be there all the time. Mind you, if he's going to take up potholing, handbags and stilettos wouldn't do her much good.

I haven't been listening, but I catch the end of what Dad's saying, ". . . then we'd stop off on Exmoor for a couple of hours, we should be there by ten if we get an early start."

Early start!

"Dad, you know you *never* get up before nine in the holidays."

"Oh well, why not break the habits of a lifetime? Wake me up at seven, and we'll hit the road before there's any traffic. We'll stop for breakfast somewhere. I've got the camping-stove in the back of the car. We'll have sausages, shall we?"

And I've got to admit it does sound quite nice. My gloom lightens. I remember when I was a kid, Dad had a little meths stove which we used to take with us on days out. That was when Dad still lived with us. We'd drive right out of London, and find somewhere with no-one else around, and he'd cook sausages or beefburgers – even chops sometimes, and I can remember him doing steak one New Year's Day. We had lots of picnics in the winter. I remember the smell of meths and smoke and frizzling meat. Mum wasn't even a vegetarian then, let alone a vegan. Dad could make camp-fires, too, with a ring of stones round the fire, and we used to stand round them, stamping our feet to keep them warm while we ate the sausages in rolls. I always burnt my mouth.

"Right, I'll wake you at six. Have you still got the meths stove we used to have?"

"No. I don't know what happened to that. Fancy you remembering it – that was years ago. It must have got lost in the move. I've got one of these little camping-gas stoves. They're much better, really."

You know how your parents are supposed to want to keep all your old stuff, like your first teeth and your first little shoe and the Mother's Day card you made when you were five? It's not like that in our house. My baby teeth got whisked away and I should think Mum probably flushed them down the toilet. She always loved her cards, but she never kept them once they'd been on the shelf for a couple of weeks. And once Dad left, everything he had of mine seemed to get lost in the move.

He keeps my letters, though. Once, when I was staying with Dad in Birmingham, I opened a drawer in the kitchen table and found a bundle of envelopes tied with a piece of string. They were all letters from me. It was funny to see them all postmarked and a bit dirty, looking quite different from how they'd been when I'd posted them.

Well, when I say bundle, it was more like a very thin sandwich. I hadn't written to him as often as I thought I had.

Dad gets up, holding our glasses.

"I'll just have another half in this," he says, "or I'll be over the limit. How about a Coke?"

Not much chance of me being over the limit on one half of shandy. But Dad's in such a good mood I don't argue, and he comes back with what looks to me like almost another full pint of Guinness, and a tall glass of Coke with lots of ice-cubes in it. I decide to strike while the iron's hot.

"Dad. After tomorrow, when we've had a day out, d'you think we could have a day at home? Just round the chalet and the bay?"

"Yes, fine," he says, not really listening. I've picked the right moment. His mind is full of maps and plans and walks and climbs and village pubs. He beams, shuts his eyes against the evening sun, and says, "This is the life, eh Colette?"

Chapter Six

AND AFTER ALL I did enjoy our day out, maps, brochures, sausages and all. Dad drove us all the way down to Exmoor, and it was nearly dark by the time we got back last night. We didn't manage to get up at six, of course, but apart from that everything went right. It wasn't like the old days with the meths stove, but it was pretty good. The sausages cooked dark brown all over, and bright pink in the middle. We had sesame buns, and ketchup, and fresh peaches and a chocolate log which Dad produced from a Coolbag he'd hidden away at the back of the boot. I made us tea, and we drank it looking right out over the Bristol Channel, so far out that the sea began to look almost blue. There were a few sheep and things, but no human beings at all. It might have been because we were so far from everything that Dad got talking, really talking. Wanting to know how I felt about things. Wanting to know what was really going on in my life. And I suppose I found it easier to talk, too, when there weren't any sounds but bees and sheep and some very high-up birds singing so fiercely you'd have thought they only lived for a day and had to get all their singing done before the night. Dad said they were larks.

We got back about ten, both of us tingling with sunburn and so tired we crashed out straight away. I don't think Dad even had a Guinness.

My sunburn's turned brown already. I looked in the mirror this morning. I washed my hair early, in the kitchen sink because the shower is hopeless, and I went out into the garden to dry it in the sun. There was a woman in the chalet garden on the other side, not the paddock side. She must have arrived the day before, because the chalet had been empty since we got there. She'd got a baby, kicking on the sheepskin rug she'd laid out on their grass. She came over to the fence to talk.

"You've got lovely hair. D'you want to borrow my hair-dryer?"

"No, it's OK. The sun'll dry it."

"I used to have mine long, before I had Sarah. I cut it when I was pregnant."

"It's a bit hot in the summer. I plait it up sometimes, so it's cooler."

"D'you ever do a French plait? It would suit you."

"My friend's mother does it sometimes."

"Would you like me to do it for you?"

I was really pleased. I got my comb and brush and stuff out of the chalet, and I went out of our gate and in through hers. She had a garden chair, so I sat in that while she did my hair. It was practically dry already, and she combed it out for a bit before she plaited it up.

"It's a lovely colour," she said. "Do you know, I always wanted to have dark hair when I was a little girl. We used to play games, pretending we were princesses, and I'd always choose to have long black hair and brown eyes."

I was watching Sarah. She kept trying to grab a tuft of grass which was just out of her reach. She was just about to crawl, Diane said. Every so often she bumped forward on her nose because she couldn't hold her head up any longer.

"How old is she?" I asked, not because I wanted to know, but because mothers always seem to talk about that kind of stuff.

"Four months. She's never seen the sea before. My husband's in Saudi, so my sister and I thought we'd get a chalet for a week."

"Oh, Saudi," I said, not really knowing what she meant, but trying to sound as if I did.

Diane laughed. "You know. Saudi Arabia. Full of rich Arabs. Dave's an engineer, that's why he's out there."

"Have you ever been there?" I asked, thinking of the travel-writing prize. Maybe Diane could win it.

"I was there for a year. I came back when I started Sarah. Dave's just finishing his contract, then we're going to live in Halifax."

"Oh, Halifax," I said, then I laughed, because I sounded like a sheep, repeating everything Diane said.

"Well, it's better than Hell or Hull, I suppose!" she said, giggling. "Your hair's lovely to work with. You could do anything with it."

"What was it like in Saudi?"

"Well, it's all right at first. You go to lots of parties with all the other Brits, but you have to be careful because alcohol's illegal there. It's against their religion. And I'd just passed my test here, but I wasn't allowed to drive."

"Why not?"

"Women can't in Saudi. So it began to feel a bit like living in a box. We had a nice flat, but it was horrible going out with men staring at you all the time. They're not used to seeing women in ordinary clothes, you see. Dave was very good, he'd drive me anywhere, but he was away working quite a lot. All the wives used to visit each other all the time. Morning coffee, afternoon tea, shopping trips. I've never eaten so many biscuits. I put on half a stone. It's a funny life. The Saudis want you there, till they've got enough of their own people trained, but you're definitely second-class. It makes you think."

"What do you mean?"

"Well, I never really thought about it before, but it made me think what it must be like to come to this country and have people thinking you're second-class, just because of what you are. Imagine anyone thinking my Sarah was second-class. I'd sock them one. But you couldn't do that in Saudi, it would have been dangerous. Keep your head still a minute. There you are. I need two mirrors really, to show you the back."

I told Diane I'd babysit for her one evening, if she and her sister wanted to go out, and went back in the house to make some breakfast for Dad and me.

That was this morning. Now I'm lying on the beach, in a quiet part just below the trees and the toll road. The sea is so far out it's just a thin line on the horizon, but there are lots of people on the beach. Families with picnic boxes and windshields and deckchairs and about six of those mats you spread out on the sand. Each family makes its own camp, then behaves exactly as if it's alone. The kids go outside the camp to build trenches and moats and towers, and to stare at the other children and maybe wish

43

they could play with them. Then they get called back to have some suntan cream put on.

I haven't got any fortifications. I haven't even got a deckchair. I've got a Japanese straw mat which rolls up and weighs practically nothing, and a book by Bruce Chatwin called ON THE BLACK HILL. I got it out of the library because I thought it would be a book about travel, and it might give me some ideas. He's a brilliant travel writer. Was. He's dead now. ON THE BLACK HILL isn't about travel at all, but I'm getting into it. I lie on my stomach and read, so that I get the shadow of my head on the page. It's nearly mid-day, and the sun's small and white and hot overhead.

Dad's gone into Weston to get himself another pair of shorts. It's much hotter than he thought it was going to be. I have an awful feeling he's going to come back with something brilliantly patterned, because that's what they've got in Marks and Spencer this year, a year after all the kids stopped wearing them. But never mind, I tell myself. What does it matter? Nobody here knows us. And Dad's kept his promise. We're not going anywhere today.

Another shadow falls across my arms.

"I thought it was you," says a voice.

I look up, blinking and squinting. It's the boy with the sandy hair and the freckles. He drops down onto the sand beside me, and sits, hugging his knees.

"Only your hair's different," he goes on. "It makes you look older."

"I am older," I say. "Older than you think."

"What're you reading?" he asks, and I turn the book round so he can see the front cover. He's never heard of Bruce Chatwin, so I tell him a bit about him.

"Sounds an interesting bloke," he says.

Suddenly I realise that we're talking, and that it hasn't been any problem starting to talk. We haven't even had to say hello or any of the other stuff about what's your name and where do you live and how old are you. We haven't had to get into the cold water inch by inch, because we're already swimming.

"We've got a lot of visitors this year," he says, eying the beach professionally.

"D'you live here, then?"

"Yes. Always have done. See those houses up there? On top of the hill? I live up there."

I follow his pointing finger and see a spiny row of roofs, high up, above the woods.

"What's it like, living here?"

He rolls over and lies on his back, shading his eyes against the sun.

"It's different in the winter," he says. "It's really quiet. You could walk all the way along this beach and not see anybody. Lots of my friends think it's dead boring. They go into Weston all the time, or up to Bristol."

"Don't you think it's boring?"

"No. It suits me. I work at the stables Saturdays, so I can ride whenever I want. And I go fishing a lot. I just like it quiet, I suppose."

"Does your friend work there, too?"

He shoots me a look.

"What, Caz? No. They wouldn't have him working with the kids. He goes out on Sheba, that's all. One of the hunters."

"Why wouldn't they have him?"

He turns away from me and scoops up some sand and lets it trickle out through his fingers.

"Listen, forget I said that. Caz wouldn't like it."

I don't say anything. We're back in cold water again. Then the boy grins at me. Somehow 'grin' is the right word for his smile. It goes with his sandy hair and his freckles and his light-green eyes.

"I don't know your name," he says. "Mine's Robert."

"I'm Colette."

"Colette. That's a nice name. I haven't heard that before. It must be a London name."

He's teasing me.

"How do you know I come from London?"

"You talk as if you do."

"Why's your friend called Caz?"

"How should I know? He just is. Always has been as far as I know."

"Is he from round here, too?"

"No. I don't know where they're from. It's not the sort of thing you ask, with Caz. They came a couple of years ago, when Caz was in the third year."

So he's fifth year now. He's still at school. He must be sixteen.

"I can guess how old you are," says Robert.

"You'll get it wrong. People always do."

"Let me see . . ." he screws up his eyes and stares hard into my face. But Robert's stare isn't the sort that makes me blush. "I estimate . . . you are approximately thirteen years and three months. Am I right?"

I can't help it, I blurt out, "How d'you know?" and he laughs and says, "We have strange powers, we who dwell by the sea. No, I asked Diane."

"Do you know Diane then?"

"I do now."

Clearly Robert has no problems starting up conversations with anybody. I bite back more questions about

46

Caz, and say, "Is there anywhere here you can get a hamburger? I'm starving."

"There was a café, but it closed. You can come up to my house if you like. I'll do you a bacon sandwich. We might even have some hamburgers in the freezer."

I hesitate. Robert's the kind of person you can't help trusting, but all the same you have to be careful. You hear horrible things, especially living in London.

Robert grins again. "It's OK," he says, "My mum's at home. She was working last night."

"What does she do?"

"She's a midwife. A sister," he says. "She usually gets up and cooks something around now.

"Are you the only one?"

"You're joking! There're five of us, and I'm the eldest. That's why Mum only works two nights. Our neighbour takes the little ones for the morning, or else I have them. But I was working up at the stables today."

"If you go round by our chalet, I can leave a note for my dad."

"Caz might call round later," says Robert casually, glancing at me. There's a laugh in his face somewhere, but with Robert it's hard to mind.

Chapter Seven

TWO LITTLE KIDS who look just like Robert are hanging over the front gate as we come up to his house. It isn't a house, it's a bungalow, but Robert says they've built an extension in the roof, where he and his next brother sleep. Robert unties the gate, which is lashed tight with plastic wire, because the baby might crawl out into the road.

"Are you sure this'll be all right?" I ask nervously. "I mean, me just turning up for a meal like this?"

"It'll be fine," says Robert. "Mum's used to it. Anyway, it'll be me cooking your hamburger, and the kids' too."

We go in through a hallway which is piled high with baby buggies, a playpen jammed against a wall, a tricycle, a bundle of free newspapers (maybe Robert does a round, like me), about fourteen empty milk-bottles, and a cardboard box full of tins of beans and extra-mammoth-size packets of cereal. Robert steps over it all and opens a door into a big room which is kitchen and living-room in one. There's a baby in a high-chair, bashing his spoon into a mess of what looks like dog-food. He has white hair sticking up straight from his head, and a big grin, like Robert's.

There's no-one else in the room, but there's a smell of toast and coffee, and a newspaper spread out on the table, as if someone's just been having breakfast. The French door through to the back garden is open.

"Mum'll be out there," says Robert. "Probably putting the washing out or something."

He moves a pile of clean, ironed T-shirts off a chair, and says, "Sit down. I'll get you a coffee – or do you like tea?"

"I'll have coffee, thanks. Robert, are you all boys?"

"Yeah. It's tough luck for Mum, isn't it? But at least we can pass the clothes down."

"Do you think she'd have liked a girl?"

"She says she's not bothered. But I think she would, really. She was a bit down when Mikey was born."

I touch Mikey's hair. It feels so soft, and the sun shines through it. You can see his scalp underneath. His cheeks are cracked, like crazy-paving.

"He's teething, aren't you, Mikey?" says Robert, and he fetches a tub of cream and rubs some into the baby's cheeks.

I can't believe my eyes when I see Robert's mother. She comes in through the French windows, swinging an empty clothes basket, and stops when she sees me. She isn't at all like the picture that has been developing inside my head ever since Robert said, "There are five of us." She's little and thin. Not a lot taller than me really. And she has dark brown curly hair, not quite as dark as mine, but pretty nearly, and one of those pointed, lively faces that never stay still for a moment. Her hair is clipped back with a comb and she's wearing a bright pink top and a little short denim skirt. She doesn't look at all like the boys. Or rather, they don't look like her. And then she grins, and it's Robert's grin.

"You must be the girl that's staying in the chalet," she says.

Robert gets very busy spooning food into Mikey. Close up, it's not so much like dog-food. I can see bits of carrot in it.

"Yes, I'm just here for a holiday, with my dad," I say.

"Oh, you'll have a great time, won't she, Robert? Some people are very hard on Weston, but there's lots to do if you look for it. You want to get Robert to show you around a bit. You'd do that, wouldn't you, Robert?"

If he would, he's not going to say so. He leaves Mikey, who squawks at being abandoned, and flips down the kettle switch. While it boils up again, he assembles mugs and coffee and a new packet of biscuits. Ginger snaps. I don't like them myself, but at the first crackle of the packet Mikey goes tense, quivering, eyes fixed on Robert.

"Will you look at him," says their mother. "But aren't you going to give the poor girl a bit more than a couple of biscuits? It's past one o'clock."

"I'm going to do hamburgers in a minute," says Robert. "Do you want me to do some for the kids?"

"That'd be great. We had a bad night, two emergency Caesarians and we were short-staffed as well. As usual. Ah well, they'll wait till there's a disaster, then they'll do something."

She sits back in a patch of sunlight and shuts her eyes. We drink our coffee without saying much. You don't have to, with the baby there to cover any awkward silences. Robert clears off the table, then gets a packet of beef-

50

burgers and some oven chips out of the freezer, and the largest tin of baked beans I've ever seen in a private house.

"Catering size," he says, catching my eye.

His mother opens her eyes.

"Oh, I'm terrible," she says. "Falling asleep in front of you. I'm not usually like this."

"No, she's not. You can count yourself lucky, Colette. She'd have had your life history out of you by now, if she hadn't been half-dead."

"I don't suppose he's even told you my name, has he? No? I thought not. It's Kathy. You've a lovely name yourself. You don't hear that one very often round here."

"I'm called after my grandma. But I don't know her, she died before I was born."

Kathy leans forward and pulls a cigarette out of the pack on the table, and lights it. Robert frowns, and says, "You're supposed to be giving that up, Mum," and she sighs and taps the cigarette on the table before lighting it, and says, "I know I am, and I will, I promise I will. It's bad enough with you and your father and Johnny on at me all the time, but now the little ones have started, I've no chance."

It seems odd to me, Kathy smoking, when she's a midwife. I mean, she must know all about what smoking does to you. But then so does Dad, and although he hides away the pack so I won't know how many he's smoked, I know he hasn't even cut down. Perhaps he can't.

"So what are you two going to do this afternoon?" asks Kathy. Robert looks at me. "Would you like to come up to the stables? D'you like riding? I could get you a free half-hour."

"I've never been on a horse," I admit, "and I haven't got any of the stuff."

"What stuff? You don't need stuff here. We just ride the horses."

"She's got to wear a hard hat," says Kathy warningly.

"Don't worry, she will. Stable rules."

I don't ask why I saw Robert and Caz riding without hard hats this morning. Perhaps it's different for them, if Robert works there.

"Is your mammy not with you, then?" asks Kathy.

"Mum!" says Robert.

"Ah, Colette doesn't mind," says Kathy. "I'm not poking my nose in, Colette. I was just wondering."

And strangely enough I don't mind Kathy wondering. She's so open about it, and her face is so alive and she's really friendly, not just pretending. And the way she said 'your mammy'. I've never heard anyone say that before.

"It's OK, Robert," I say, "I don't mind. My mum and dad don't live together any more. They're divorced."

"I thought that might be it," says Kathy, "when Robert said there was just the two of you down here on holiday. It must be nice, to have your dad to yourself for a bit. I know that was what I always wanted, when I was about your age."

"Mm," I agree. "Yes, it is."

"Is your mum in London, then?" asks Robert.

"Yes. She's taking her holiday later, at the end of the month. We're going camping with some friends."

"God, you're lucky!" says Robert. "Two holidays!"

He says it with such feeling that I'm a bit embarrassed. And Kathy's face suddenly goes still, and she says, "I keep telling you, you ought to keep some of your money for yourself. You could go off youth hostelling with some of your friends. Or camping."

"What would I need to go on holiday for?" asks

Robert. "People pay to come here for their holidays, don't they?"

"Well, that's true, they do," agrees Kathy, relaxing.

"Besides," Robert goes on, separating the frozen hamburgers with a knife. "There's no hurry. But you wait till I'm eighteen. Then I'll hit the road."

"Once you're eighteen, you're going to college," says Kathy firmly. "You're the only one of the lot who's any good at school, so we can't waste you."

"There's no way I'm going straight to college, Mum. I want a year off. Travelling. Working abroad maybe. I'll need to get some money together, too. People say a grant goes nowhere."

"I can hear Caz talking," says Kathy.

All this time, Robert has been moving quickly and deftly from fridge to cooker to table. The chips are in the oven, the beans in the pan, and the burgers are under the grill. The smell of food fills the kitchen, and a couple of minutes later the two little boys burst in and ask when they're going to get something to eat.

"You can have yours in the garden," says Robert, and he splits some burger buns for them. In a few more minutes he's got a plate of food organised for each of us. I'm impressed. Everything's cooked just right, and he's even managed to make us more coffee at the same time. I bite into my burger and my mouth fills with saliva. I'm really hungry.

We're all forking up the last of our chips when there's a knock at the back door. I glance up, expecting to see the little boys after more ketchup, but it's a taller, darker shape against the glass. Caz.

Robert's delighted, but Kathy's face goes still and shadowy again. Her face is amazing. How does she hide anything she's thinking? She certainly hasn't hidden anything from Caz. While Robert's pressing food and coffee on him, he glances at Kathy, and then sits down quietly, refusing food and drink. I feel self-conscious, eating while Caz sits there. A glob of ketchup runs down my chin and I wipe it off hastily, and put my knife and fork together, pretending I don't want any more even though I'm still hungry and could eat another plateful.

"Which will you have, Colette, an apple or an orange?" asks Kathy.

I weigh up the crunching and chomping of the apple against the slurping of the orange and lie, "I don't really like fruit much, thank you, Kathy."

"Would you like something else? A chocolate biscuit maybe?"

"No, really, that was great. I've had enough. Thank you."

Robert picks two dark green apples out of the paper bag in the vegetable rack. He washes them, and he and Kathy eat their apples, crunching into the white flesh which is fizzing with juice. The juice runs down over Kathy's chin but she just laughs and wipes it off with a finger and says, "Ooh, this is the best apple I've had for ages. Are you sure you won't have one, Colette?"

My mouth tingles with longing, but I refuse.

All the time I feel as if Caz is watching me. He isn't really, or at least, whenever I look round, he isn't. He reaches over and picks up Mikey, who's starting to grizzle, and jumps him on his lap. Mikey loves it. He goes right over the top, grinning and shrieking and trying to seize lumps of Caz's hair. Then all at once it gets too much for him and his face crumples up and he starts to cry, arching his back and wailing miserably while his face goes from pink to almost purple.

"Give him here," says Kathy. "He's ready for his sleep."

It's a while before she emerges from Mikey's little bedroom, saying grimly, "That's babies for you, Colette. Easy to wind up, but not so easy to wind down again."

Meanwhile not much conversation has taken place between Robert and Caz and myself. Robert's all right, because he's got the washing-up to do. I ask if I can help, but he says no, so I sit there, finishing off my coffee and trying to think of something to say.

"We're going up to the stables this afternoon," I say in the end.

"You riding?" asks Caz, speaking more to Robert than to me.

"Not really," says Robert. "It's Colette's first time."

"There's always a first time, isn't there," said Caz. "For everything."

And he gives me a sudden smile, not a grin but a smile, one that seems to make his eyes liquid. One that makes my stomach go liquid. It doesn't last for more than a second, though, and we're back where we started. I'm relieved when Kathy comes back. It's impossible to stay silent when she's around, and even Caz talks quite normally, if you can say normally when they're actually talking about an unsolved murder that took place around here years ago. It comes up because Caz starts talking about dogs, and how if their master or mistress gets killed they'll stay by the body, no matter what. For weeks, even. It sounds horrible, and Caz goes on and on. More to stop him than because I'm interested, I ask, "How old was she?

The girl I mean?" in a voice which comes out stupidly little and frightened.

Caz looks at me consideringly for a long moment before replying, "About your age."

"Or about your age, for God's sake, Caz Smith," says Kathy crossly. "The poor girl's come here for her holidays, she doesn't want to hear all that old stuff."

There's a silence, during which I imagine worse things than the ones I've just been told. I'd rather know the whole story, always. At least then you're prepared.

"Coming out tonight, Rob?" asks Caz.

"Might do," says Robert, equally casual.

"I'll pick up the bait then."

"We go fishing when the tide's right," Robert explains to me. "You can come along if you like."

"Colette's not going night-fishing with you two," says Kathy, calmly but definitely, and although Robert grimaces at me, I'm glad. Even though Mum drives me bananas with her animal rights leaflets and the fact she won't even wear leather shoes any more, I agree with her about hunting and fishing and things like that. Or perhaps I'm afraid that I'd enjoy it, and what would that say about me?

"See you later, then," says Caz.

Chapter Eight

THE KITCHEN RELAXES once Caz has gone. Robert goes to fetch me a pair of his brother Johnny's jeans to go riding in. You can't ride in shorts, he says. The jeans fit me, which is disappointing as Johnny is a year younger than me. I've got all the names now. Robert, Johnny, Stevie and Paul, Mikey. No sign of Robert's dad, but he does exist. There's a big waterproof fishing coat on the back of the kitchen door to prove it.

The stables are owned by an enormous square woman called Dot. The first part of her I see is her backside, straining in tight off-white jodphurs as she bends over a tiny kid who's whingeing and refusing to be put on a pony.

"Oh it's you, Robert, thank goodness," booms Dot. "You can take over for me."

So I spend half an hour or so watching Robert get this kid to the point of sitting on the pony and beaming as the pony walks carefully round in circles. Robert talks to the kid all the time, in the same voice as he uses to the pony. The mother turns up for the last ten minutes of the lesson and watches what's going on with a critical expression.

When Robert brings them round to her she says, "I'm sure you know what you're doing, but I did think she'd be getting on a bit faster than this."

Robert starts to explain what he's doing in the same pony/kid voice. Eventually the mother agrees that perhaps he does know what he's doing, especially as the kid looks at Robert adoringly the whole time and says, "Mummy, I only want *this* boy to help me when I come here."

The kid is dressed up in tiny jodphurs and jacket and hard hat already, before it's even learned to ride.

When they've gone, Robert takes all the stuff off the pony and leads it into one of the paddocks. Then he comes and flops down on the grass beside me.

"What an awful woman," I say. "Are they all like that?"

Robert shrugs. "You always get a few. Usually the private-lesson ones. But most of the parents drop their kids off at the gates. We couldn't have parents milling round on Saturday mornings. D'you still want to have a go?"

I say I do, and for the next half-hour I don't have time to think. For a start, the horse is so much wider than you imagine. It's like sitting across a table-top, and it hurts muscles in your legs you didn't know you had. I call it a horse, but Robert calls it a nice old pony, just the right size for you, Colette, and not an ounce of badness in her. But even the best pony puts her head down so you feel you're going to shoot down her neck and land under her hooves. Even the best pony is hot and prickly and makes you feel it's alive and might do anything. I put the reins round my fingers as Robert shows me, and hold on much too tight until he tells me this isn't a white-knuckle ride. My knees won't grip the pony's sides the way they ought to, and as for making the pony do anything, I can't believe she'd take the slightest bit of notice.

And then she does. I dig my heels in, the way Robert tells me to, and suddenly the pony's walking forward, in its rolling, table-top way, and I'm not only staying on it, but I'm enjoying it. I feel as good as if I was tearing down the straight in the Grand National. I'm on a pony. I'm really riding. Brilliant!

By the time I get off, I'm exhausted. I go round to the pony's head and stroke her nose and say, "Thanks, Heidi, that was great."

She noses about to see if I've got anything for her to eat, then gives up and attacks a clump of grass instead, chomping through it with her big yellow teeth.

"I could get you another ride," says Robert, "maybe on Saturday, after I've finished my lessons? I'd have to clear it with Dot, but it'll be OK."

"I don't mind paying," I say.

"No, you're not paying. She lets Caz come up here and ride Sheba all the time. God knows why. Dot hunts in the winter – Sheba's her own mare. She's a funny old bag."

"Who, Sheba?"

Robert grins. "No, Dot. She's funny about Caz. *I've got a soft spot for that young man. Sheba's never been in such good condition.*"

"She sounds a bit of a snob, when she talks."

"She's all right. It's just her manner. It's not like London, down here. Riding's not such a snob thing. There's hundreds of stables, livery, you name it. You want to come up on a Saturday and see the kids who go riding."

I look at my watch. It's quarter to five, and I haven't seen Dad since the morning.

"D'you want to come down and have tea with us?" I ask.

Robert hesitates, then he says, "No, thanks all the same. I'd better get back."

But I feel that's not the real reason.

We're walking slowly down the hill together, talking about the wages Robert gets from working at the stables, when we hear hooves behind us. As we turn around, I feel I know who it's going to be. And it is. Caz. On a big dark glossy horse. Mare. Not the horse I saw him ride into the sea. I know nothing about horses, but even I can tell the difference between this one and the others I've seen. Caz stops beside us, and I feel small and vulnerable next to the mare's legs and her heavy hooves. The sunlight shines blue on her sides, which are such a dark brown they're almost black. She shifts from hoof to hoof, as if she doesn't know what to do with the energy that's simmering just under her skin. A couple of flies land near her eyes and she flicks her head and jitters. Caz doesn't look as if he's just sitting on the mare. He looks like part of her. The mare glances at me sidelong out of her dark, shining eyes, and it's not a casual glance. She looks through me and sums me up. I know what she is saying: *Who's the stronger? Who's going to get her own way? You or me?* And I know the answer.

"Did you get on all right, Colette?" Caz asks me, and I answer, "Fine."

Sheba moves again, a sideways rippling movement, and her hooves strike on the hard road.

"I'll take you out some time," says Caz. "When you're ready."

"That *will* be some time, then," says Robert, and I find I'm angry with him, not with Caz.

Caz rides on down the hill, and we trudge after him like a couple of peasants following the lord's horse in the middle ages.

Robert's frowning. The easiness of the day has gone. When we get to where the road forks, Robert stops and turns to me and says, "You don't want to take a lot of notice of Caz, Colette. I get on with him all right, because I know what to expect with him. But it takes a while to get to know someone like Caz."

I bristle a bit. Doesn't Robert realise I've spent most of my life dodging weirdos in the park and on the Tube? London's full of them.

"He seems perfectly normal to me," I say.

Apart from being the best-looking person I've ever set eyes on, that is.

"He's had a hard time," says Robert.

"How do you mean?"

"He's been here a couple of years, and that's the longest he's lived anywhere. Or since his mother died, anyway."

"When did she die?"

"When Caz was nine. A long time before they came here. His old man can't cope, so he keeps moving. He got this caravan down on the bay, and when Caz first came to our school he was supposed to be moving on at the end of the summer, but this time they've stayed."

"Has his father got a job?"

"Yeah, he's had lots of jobs. This one won't last long. He works in the amusement arcade on the pier. But he's a boozer. And he's got a terrible temper on him, like Caz, but he can't control it. So the job won't last."

I can't think of much to say. I try to imagine what it

must be like, living in that caravan with a father who drinks and can't keep a job.

"Caz ought to get out of it!" says Robert suddenly and quite fiercely.

"But what could he do? He's only sixteen, isn't he?"

"Caz's got the brains to do anything, if he wants. He could get away to college, get a good job, get himself out of all this. If his old man'd let him."

"Wouldn't he?"

"Well, he might. He's not all bad. He's quite a bright bloke, really, only nothing's gone right for him. Caz said once, it kicked his dad in when his mother died. He doesn't know how to go about doing anything for Caz. And Caz won't listen to anyone who *does* know. His Head of Year really likes Caz, God knows why when you think of the trouble he's caused, and he said he'd coach Caz out of school in Maths and Physics, for nothing, because he'd missed so much with moving. It worked out all right for a while, and Caz was doing really well, then he just dropped it and wouldn't go any more. He started taking Sheba out all the time instead. He won't let himself get anywhere."

"Did he do his GCSEs?"

"Yeah, he did them. But he could have done really well. Anyway, never mind. It's not your problem."

It isn't, but I wish it was. Now Robert seems to regret having told me so much. He makes me promise not to let anything slip in front of Caz, not about his mother, or anything. Caz wouldn't like me to know.

"I wouldn't want you to get on the wrong side of Caz," says Robert.

And nor would I.

"See you tomorrow?" says Robert as I turn to go. It's half a question, half a statement.

"All right. But I'll have to check what my dad wants to do first."

"I'll come round about ten, then."

"I'll give you the jeans back," I say. I'm still wearing them over my shorts. "Thanks for the riding, and the hamburgers and everything."

"Oh, that's all right. Any time," says Robert, and unlike most people who say this sort of thing, he sounds as if he means it. I watch him walk off, quite quickly, towards the bungalow, whistling. What's he going to do now? Give Mikey a bath? Cook bacon sandwiches for the seven of them? Do his paper-round?

No. He's going night-fishing with Caz. A cloud of jealousy blows across my liking for Robert. It's an ugly feeling, and trying to shake it off, I run down the hill towards our chalet.

Chapter Nine

DAD'S HAD A long, quiet sunny day to himself. He's gone into Weston and bought the kind of shorts I thought he'd buy. But they aren't too bad. He's had lunch in a pub, then he's taken the newspaper and his cigarettes and a deckchair that goes with the chalet, and lain out on the beach all afternoon. He's had the kind of day with not a thing that needs to be done and no phone ringing and no bills to pay, which adults are always saying they'd give their right arm for.

And he's completely fed up. I realise this when I'm about half-way through telling him all about Robert and Robert's family and the stables and Heidi. For some reason, I don't tell him anything about Caz. He says, "That sounds like fun," and "I'm glad you had a good time," and I grind to a halt, because his voice is so flat and in a way sad, though I'm sure he's not making it like that on purpose.

"Your suntan's coming on, Dad," I say encouragingly. "I like the shorts."

Why is it that as soon as I'm with a member of my family, lies start pouring out?

And why is it that the people you love most in the world can make you want to run as far as you can in the opposite direction?

For a few moments I stand by his deckchair, which he's moved back into the chalet garden, and dream of a Europass Rail Ticket. Trains running through Alpine passes in the middle of the night. Me waking up and twitching the blind aside and seeing the moon reflected on the snow, and nothing but forest and jagged mountain peaks. Or is that shadow a wolf, running alongside the coach then dropping back as I curl up warmly in my bunk and the train lets out a hoot before it thunders into a tunnel?

Back in real life, Dad rubs his forehead.

"I've got a bit of a headache," he says. "I'll have a couple of paracetamol, then we can think about what we want to do this evening."

"You shouldn't lie out in the sun so long," I say, not adding *when you've been drinking at lunchtime*.

We don't do much that evening. We go for a walk up on Sand Point and get chased by two horses. Robert's right, they're all over the place, as common as cats in London. Then we come back for a drink on the pub terrace. When we get home, we make coffee and wander out into the garden. Dad's still not very cheerful, so I'm not spoiling anything when I say, "Dad – about tomorrow. You know the boy I was telling you about? Robert? He said he'd come round about ten."

"What? Ten in the morning?"

I sigh.

"Of course, ten in the morning. He wouldn't be coming round at ten at night, would he?"

"Look, is this boy Robert going to be a permanent feature of this holiday? I only ask."

"Oh Dad, don't be like that. He's not a boyfriend or anything. He's just nice. He's going to show me round Weston a bit."

At this point I see Diane over the fence. She's not listening or anything, just bobbing up and down picking the baby's things off the grass, but Dad's talking so loudly she can't be missing much.

"Show you round Weston a bit! Well, I don't know," says Dad. Then in the voice of someone who genuinely wants to know, he asks, "Are you like this at your mother's?"

"Like what?"

"Well, I don't really know how to put it, Colette. I mean, always knowing what you want to do and then doing it."

I can scarcely believe my ears. Little does Dad know, if he calls this doing what I want.

"Oh, I'm not blaming you," he adds quickly. "You're growing up. It's natural. It's just I'm not used to it. You'll have to give me time to adjust."

"Well," I say cautiously, "I suppose, in London, kids my age go out more than they do in Birmingham. I mean, Mum doesn't mind as long as she knows where I'm going and who I'm with."

There are certain issues between Mum and me which I don't feel like mentioning at this moment. Groundings. Curfews. Major rows over friends like Claudia. For about six weeks I thought Claudia was so wonderful I wanted to do everything she did. And with Claudia, that was quite a lot.

"*Her parents just bring Claudia in with the milk,*" they said at school.

"And what am I supposed to do with myself tomorrow, while you're swanning round Weston?" asks Dad in a would-be humorous voice that makes me curl up inside. I almost say, 'I won't go, Dad. I'd rather be with you.'

I'm getting to the point now when I don't know what's a lie and what isn't.

But I don't. Instead, I say, "It'll only be for the morning, Dad. Then let's go down to Brean, like you said."

Robert makes a good impression the next morning. For a start, he's got Mikey with him in the buggy. Dad's quite amused, and I can tell he likes Robert. I'd never thought that Dad liked babies, but he takes Mikey out of the buggy and swings him up on his shoulders and says, "Let's find this young man a biscuit," while Robert and I look at each other. We hear Dad whistling then singing in the kitchen, and Mikey babbling, then after a while Dad comes down with Mikey tucked under one arm and clutching a biscuit. Dad's got a couple of mugs in his free hand, and he passes them to Robert and me, saying, "I hope coffee's all right, Robert."

While we drink it he asks Robert about his family — all the stuff I've already told him, in fact, and then we agree what time I'm coming back, and Dad hands back the baby.

It feels really strange, walking off beside Robert, with the baby in his buggy. Dad waves, then picks up his paper.

"Don't worry," says Robert, "we're not stuck with Mikey the whole morning. I'm giving Mum half an hour to sort out Stevie. He's in a terrible mood this morning. Throwing things. He's jealous of Mikey, really. I'll just get the bread at the shop then we'll take him back."

"How did your fishing go?" I ask.

"Not so great," says Robert. "Is that the time? I said we'd meet Caz by the toll booth at eleven. Come on."

It's true, your heart does beat faster with excitement. And Mikey is shrieking with joy as we bounce him over the potholes, tear into the shop to fetch the bread, and back up the hill. Kathy's throwing balls to Stevie in the garden. The cricket bat is much too big for him, but he manages to hit one ball back just as we come in through the gate, which means he has to rush up to Robert shouting, "Did you see that?"

Kathy looks a bit fed up. When she says to us, "Have a nice time now," she comes right to the gate and stands looking down the road, with Mikey slung on her hip, as if she'd like to come too.

I think of Dad reading his newspaper in the chalet garden, and of Kathy playing cricket with the little ones in the bungalow garden.

"It seems stupid, doesn't it?" I say aloud.

"What?"

"Oh – your mother and my dad, one in each garden. Both of them wishing we weren't going out. You know, my dad would really enjoy playing cricket with Stevie and Paul. Everyone in their separate lives, I suppose that's what I mean."

"Well, that's what it's like, isn't it? You can't do anything about it."

"And there's Diane as well. She's on her own with Sarah. Her husband's in Saudi, you know."

I feel quite pleased with myself, saying 'in Saudi' like that, as if I've known all about Saudi for ages.

"Mum'll be fine," says Robert. "My dad's taking this

afternoon off, so they'll probably go out and take the little ones for a picnic."

This is the first definite mention of Robert's father. I'm quite curious. I wonder if he's like Kathy, or like Robert. Like Robert, I think. You couldn't have two Kathys in one house. Or bungalow.

"What does he do, your father?"

"He teaches the fiddle."

"Fiddle?" Wild visions of fraud and bank robbery seethe through my mind. "What sort of fiddle?"

Robert raises his right arm and draws a quick, expert bow across the air.

"Oh – *violin*. He must be good, if he teaches it."

"Yeah, he is. He plays in a band as well. An Irish band. They play traditional music. He goes round schools, as well. Peripatetic teaching, it's called. But he wouldn't work in a school, he says he doesn't like the atmosphere."

"Who does?"

"And he has pupils who come to the house. Poor devils. He makes them work."

"Do you play the violin?"

"Well, I do and I don't. Dad started me when I was about five. I was the first, so he was quite enthusiastic, but you could soon tell I wasn't going to be that great. I mean, I can play. I like the Irish fiddle music. But I'm no good from Dad's point of view. Now Johnny is, he's really good, but he messes around."

"Like Caz."

"Yes. There's a lot of it about. Those that can, won't. Or not properly. Mind you, Dad forces Johnny, because he knows he's got it in him. So much practice a day, or no pocket money and you're not going out on Friday night, that sort of thing."

"Does it bother you, not being good at it?"

"No, not any more. It used to. I used to think, God, I'm useless at everything. You know how you do."

"Yes."

"It got better when I stopped trying. I didn't play at all for a year, then I started again, just playing the music I like, not killing myself over it any more."

We stop and sit on a low wall by the toll-booth, waiting for Caz. I stretch my legs into the sun and think about what Robert has said. In a way, although they're completely different, Robert reminds me of Angelina. Of all my friends, Angelina is the one who thinks things through, works out what to do and then does it, while the rest of us are more like people trying to cross a river on stepping-stones, jumping wildly from one to the next. The stones aren't very firm and they're slippery and it's always much farther than you think to the next one.

Why is it that Caz always appears as if from nowhere? One minute I'm sitting there with my eyes half-shut, blissfully warm and comfortable, then the next Caz is standing in front of me. Black T-shirt with white logo, black jeans. He starts telling Robert about an arm-wrestling contest he's seen in the pub last night. "He had his arm like this – here, give us your arm, Robert – " and Robert does, and in a minute they're straining and sweating with their arms locked, each trying to force the other's arm down. The sharp stone top of the wall digs into their elbows, and small beads of sweat break out on Robert's forehead. I don't like it. I back off a little, and say, "I thought we were going into Weston."

As if a spell has been broken, both of them look up, lose their concentration, and the match is over. Robert rubs his right arm. "That's my bowing arm, you sod," he says, but he's smiling. The heaviness has gone out of the atmosphere.

But I have a feeling it's not going to be a restful morning, and I'm right. We go into Weston by the toll road, which takes us about twenty minutes. Now Robert and Caz are great mates again, and I'm the one on the edge. But at least Robert remembers I'm there, and points things out to me and tells me about them. As far as Caz is concerned, I'm scarcely visible. Except once, when he says my French plait reminds him of the way they plait horses' manes for shows.

But as he says it, he comes close and runs a finger down the plait, and says, softly, "I like women with long hair."

And I just don't know how to handle this. One part of me is flattered. No-one has called me a woman before. Another part wants to bleat, 'I'm only thirteen.'

But I needn't worry. Robert does it for me, and I'm furious. I actually blush with rage.

"Colette's only thirteen, Caz," he says, very calmly but as if it's a warning.

We go down to the pier, because I say I want to go on the arcade. Really, I want to see what Caz's father looks like. But he isn't there, and we soon get tired of shovelling 10p pieces into the machines in the hope that one of them will topple over the edge and release a silver waterfall of coins into our greedy hands. Just as we're on our way out, Caz says, "One last try," and puts in a 10p and to our astonishment there's a gathering rattle of coins and the whole dirty used pile of them comes down into the drawer beneath the machine. We grab and count feverishly. The machine rake goes forward and more money overbalances and topples down. We need both hands to scoop it out.

"Will you look at this!"

"Jeez!"

"Brilliant!"

We have £8.40. It's not so amazing, really, but it feels like Christmas there for a minute. We decide immediately that we're going to waste the money on something we'd never have done otherwise, if we hadn't won it.

"God!" says Caz. "We'll take Colette to the ice-cream parlour."

And they do. I can hardly believe it, because I'd have thought Caz would want to do some hard man stuff like buying lager with it. But he's going on about knickerbocker glories and peach melba and banana splits and raspberry sauce and I can't wait.

Chapter Ten

THE ICE-CREAM parlour isn't anything like I thought it would be. We turn into a little side street, and duck down a flight of steps into a low creamy-white room. At first it looks as if every table's full, but there's one left in the corner, by the enormous mirror that runs the length of the back wall. You can queue at the counter for cornets to take away, or sit at the tables and be served by waitresses, who are dressed like old-fashioned waitresses, in black with white caps. But they're young, only a few years older than me. Students, I expect. One of them slaps down the menu in front of Caz, and I look around while he studies it.

The people on the table next to us have just had their order served. My mouth waters as I try not to stare too hard at the mound of banana with raspberry sauce and ice-cream and cream topping in one boat-shaped glass; the tall glass layered with peach, strawberry and pink and white ice-cream: and the rich dark chocolate swirl with a flake sticking out of it in the third dish. A big sign by the counter says that all the ice-cream is freshly made on the premises.

Caz is reading the menu aloud.

"*Knickerbocker Glory, Coup Italienne, Peach Surprise, Ski Sundae, Golden Acacia Honey Waltzer, Mocha Slice . . .*"

"What's in the Coup Italienne?" asks Robert.

"*Layers of creamy Neapolitan ice-cream and fresh nectarines, topped with home-made vanilla sauce and toasted almonds.*"

"I'll have that. How much is it?"

"£2.25."

I choose the Golden Acacia Honey Waltzer, because I love honey and ginger. Caz has Mocha Slice: "*Rich dark chocolate and pale coffee, made from real coffee-beans, flavoured with rum and topped with whipped cream.*"

We have to wait a bit before the ice-creams come, but it's worth it. It must be the best ice-cream I've ever tasted, and I've tasted a lot of ice-cream. There are slivers of fresh ginger in mine, and slices of tangerine. We eat them very slowly, digging in with our long spoons and lingering over every mouthful.

The bill comes to £7.40. Money well spent, we agree, staggering out of the shop.

But after this, things get difficult again. We go down to the beach, but the sea's miles out and the mud smells raw. Caz and Robert stand around hurling stones into the deep mud under the pier. It starts off friendly, but it turns into a competition again. Then they both come and sit down by me. Caz looks bored. He stares out at the invisible sea. He looks as if he's had enough of this outing. I search around frantically for something to say. Something interesting, something funny, something which will make Caz turn to me and smile. But nothing comes.

"What are you doing tomorrow?" Robert asks him.

"Going caving with a couple of mates. Want to come along?"

But the way Caz says it doesn't sound very pleasant, and Robert answers sharply, "No thanks. You know how I feel about caves."

"Why don't you do something about it? You're really missing out!" says Caz. "You've got to fight these things."

Robert doesn't answer. He looks really angry. It makes it worse that I'm here, listening to it all. Caz goes on, "It's like people who hate spiders. They do these courses. Aversion therapy. By the end of the course they're stroking tarantulas."

"What would anybody want to stroke a tarantula for?" I say, trying to break the tension, but this time Robert replies quite coolly, "Everybody's got something they can't deal with, Caz. Heights, or water, or spiders, or lifts or whatever. Even you. For me it's going underground, and you know that and we've talked about it so let's shut up about it now, shall we?"

Caz is silent, then he smiles at Robert. There might be an apology in the smile, but I'm not sure. He turns to me.

"How about you, Colette? Have you done any caving?"

I shake my head. I wish I had Robert's guts. I wish I could just say straight out, "I don't like going underground. I'm afraid."

But I can't. Caz starts telling me about caving and I find myself making interested noises and saying how exciting it sounds. Robert gives me a look. I'm pretty sure he knows just how interesting and exciting I truly think it sounds. Caz tells me about how sometimes you find your way blocked by water coming right up to the roof. It's called a sump. If you have a guide, you'll know how long the water goes on for, and you free-dive your way through it. Sometimes there are pockets of air up against the roof, but you have to be careful in case the air's bad. The passages get so narrow you have to wriggle your way through. Caz says they call them squeeze passages.

It sounds like all my worst nightmares come true, and they call it sport. I try to imagine squeezing my body into a narrow, wet passage hundreds of feet underground. You get jammed sometimes, Caz says, but as long as you don't panic you'll be OK. If you can get your arm and your head through, the rest of your body will go after it. The only problem is that when people panic they swell up a bit and that makes it more difficult for them to free themselves.

I hope that I'm managing to keep an expression of horror and disbelief off my face.

Robert's really interested. "You know, Caz," he says, "it sounds to me as if you're describing being born. Do you think that's why people get hooked on it? They're going through the experience of being born, over and over. Perhaps that's what they're hung up on."

This stops Caz for a while. He thinks it over, and I'm expecting him to rubbish what Robert's said, but he doesn't. He gives Robert a slow, acknowledging grin and says, "There might be something in that. You're glad to see daylight after a long squeeze, I can tell you."

It seems that you need quite a lot of equipment. Helmets. Boots. Wetsuits with knee pads. It costs a lot. I remember the three men Dad and I saw, crossing the field then disappearing down that wet hole.

"But you wouldn't need all that stuff, Colette," says Caz. "If I took you, we'd do something easy. I can borrow a helmet for you."

"I couldn't go through one of those squeezes," I admit. "It makes me feel sick thinking about it."

"You'd be all right. Once you're down there, you don't have time to think about it. You just think about the next move."

He's really enthusiastic. I haven't seen Caz like this, and it's quite a revelation. His eyes aren't just liquid, they glow as well, and he makes you feel as if you're the only other person in the world. The only one who matters.

"We'd better be getting back, Colette," says Robert. "Your dad's expecting you at half-past-one."

"Oh. Yes." I drag my attention away from Caz, but he isn't going to let me go that easily.

"How about it, then?" he asks urgently. "I could take you Saturday."

"Your club won't want to be bothered with Colette," says Robert. "They don't take novices, do they?"

"Oh, I'll drive her across in Dad's van and we'll do something easy," says Caz.

Drive me across? How can Caz drive a van when he's only sixteen?

"You can't take her on her own," said Robert, "her Dad wouldn't like it. Anyway, you don't really want to go, do you, Colette?"

I look out at the wide open horizon and the lumpy outline of Brean Down. The sky's pale and clear above me, and there are several seagulls swinging around the end of the pier. Who'd want to leave all this and go into a wet, dark, narrow passage underground?

"I'd like to give it a try," I say. As I say it, my heart gives a swoop as if I'm going down in a lift very fast, then steadies itself into a hot, tight ball under my ribs.

"Right. Saturday then. I'll pick you up in the morning,

about nine? We'll be back by dinnertime. You'd better not tell your dad where you're going though. Robert's right, he'd only worry."

"I don't think you should take her on her own," repeats Robert stubbornly.

"You want to come along, too, then?" flashes Caz. "The offer's open."

Caz is staying in town to see a film with some friends, so I walk back with Robert. Or rather, walk and run, because we're quite late and I don't want to upset Dad again. Robert doesn't say much, but I have the feeling that he's got quite a lot to say, and is saving it up for another time, when he's got more breath. We part a couple of hundred yards from the chalet.

"You want to come up to our house later?" asks Robert.

"I'd like to, but I'm not sure what Dad's got planned," I say.

"Here, this is my phone number," says Robert, scribbling it on the back of the ice-cream parlour bill. "Phone me before six if you're coming."

We say goodbye. Just as I'm going, Robert looks as if he's going to start to say something else. I feel sure he's going to tell me why I shouldn't go caving with Caz, so I wave and smile and say, "God, is that the time? I'll have to rush. See you later."

As it turns out I needn't have worried. This time Dad's not lying about in a deckchair, nursing a headache and feeling sorry for himself. I can hear voices as I come up to the chalet gate. There's a big red and white checked cloth spread across our lawn, and Dad and Diane and another blonde girl, younger than Diane, who must be her sister. Sarah's on her sheepskin as usual, lying on her back this time, catching hold of her toes.

Dad waves as I come in through the gate.

"You're just in time, Colette!" he calls. "We decided to have a picnic!"

There he is, having a lovely time without me. Just what I wanted. Just what I thought I wanted, anyway. I look at the blonde sister, who's wearing a crimson halter-neck T-shirt which shows off her brown back and arms, and khaki shorts which do the same for her legs. She's laughing and eating at the same time, showing very white teeth. Then she smiles at me, and I see she's got a real smile, just like Diane's. Never mind about the tan and the blonde hair and the boobs. She's all right.

They've got French bread and ham and tomatoes and cheese with holes in it and salad and coleslaw and white wine. There's a heap of peaches on a plate, and Danish pastries. Dad's been off to the big supermarket in Worle to buy all these goodies, and Diane's brought the wine. It's a pity I ate so much ice-cream. I'm not really hungry.

"Colette, this is Paula," says Diane, and we smile and say hello.

"Do you drink wine, Colette?" asks Paula.

I say I'll have it with mineral water. I get a headache if I drink wine in the sun. She pours me a glass, and the sparkling water fizzes over the top of the bottle into the peaches. They look lovely with drops of water on them, as if they've just come off the tree.

There's a lot of talking and laughing and making plans. Paula and Diane haven't got a car. Paula had to get a taxi from the station, which makes Dad cross because he says Diane ought to have asked him. They agree that we'll all have a day out together. What about Cheddar? Have the girls seen the caves there? They haven't, and it's agreed that we'll all go on Sunday.

"And if you need to do a big shop for the week, I'll take you round to Sainsbury's," says Dad.

"That's OK, there's a bus that goes from the village," says Diane. "The woman in the post office told me."

Dad says that it's ridiculous for them to be carting stuff about on the bus when there's a car right next door. Paula says she thinks they'll live on salad and pizzas, anyway. She for one doesn't feel like doing any cooking on holiday.

"Holiday!" teases Diane. "You have so many holidays I can't keep up with them."

It turns out that Paula works for a package holiday company. She gets cheap flights plus free holidays when they're checking out new resorts.

"Don't call them holidays!" says Paula. "I've never worked so hard in my life as I did in Turkey last year. We're opening up a new part of the coast there. The temperature was over a hundred every day."

"You ought to talk to Colette," says Dad. "She fancies travelling."

I don't say that package holidays aren't the kind of travel I want to do. *Colette Byrne, our correspondent in Benidorm.*

But Turkey sounds interesting, and I start to ask Paula about it.

"Oh it's lovely at the moment," she says. "Just like the brochures. Except that by the time we've written the brochures it won't be like that any more. There're so many hotels going up it'll be like Legoland in ten years."

It's nice of Paula to come on holiday to Sand Bay with

her sister when she could be in Turkey or Cyprus. But you can tell that she and Diane like each other. And Paula can't leave baby Sarah alone. She's always picking her up and cuddling her and breaking off what she's saying to exclaim, "Look at Sarah! She nearly got that rattle all on her own!"

And Diane's only too delighted to have her sister take over Sarah. When you think of it, it must be hard for Diane, without anybody else there who's interested in what Sarah does or whether she might have crawled six inches today or not.

Dad's happy as a clam. He keeps filling up people's glasses, and cutting more slices of French bread. He does remember to ask, "Did you and Robert have a good morning?" and I just tell him, yes, fine, and he goes back to offering cigarettes and laughing as Paula tells stories about trying to make deals with Turkish hoteliers who don't speak English, and her own attempts to use the Turkish she's learned from a tape.

"He looked a bit surprised and later on I realised what I'd been saying meant '*I always love to see your insides*'."

I can see the party's going to go on all afternoon. Tea and coffee come out, and later someone suggests a paddle, because the tide's going to be up at four. I feel very tired. I say to Dad that I'm going inside for a bit, because I've had enough sun. I think I might read, but the print hurts my eyes, and I lie down on my bed and listen to the sounds of laughter and talking and far-off sounds of the beach. I shut my eyes.

I have the dream again. It's a bit like one I often have, but this time it's worse. I'm in Turkey, on a caving holiday, with a group of cavers who don't realise I've never done it before. I try to tell them but nobody's listening. Then we're in a cave and someone's saying, "Super Severe, Super Severe," over and over. I'm walking down a narrow passage, hurrying, because it's dark behind me. All the others have gone, but I hear footsteps behind me. I go faster. I'm nearly running now, and I trip, and bang my head. The roof's getting lower. I crouch, and run on. The passage is getting narrower and narrower. I have to crawl, then the rock is pressing in on all sides of me and I'm wriggling, trying to force my way through. There aren't any footsteps behind me now, but I can hear someone breathing, heavy, huffing breath, more like an animal than a human being. Then a hand snaps around my left ankle, and grips it. I kick out, but it's no good, and I can't turn round. I can only go on, dragging whatever it is that's got hold of my foot. Then a voice starts saying behind me,

"It's going to be a tight squeeze, Colette, it's going to be a tight squeeze," and I scream because the rock is shutting in front of me and I wake up.

I'm sweating. My T-shirt sticks to me. My face is pressed hard against the pillow, and I'm making a sobbing noise. I've never heard myself making that noise before.

I lie still, until my breathing returns to normal and the noise stops. I feel shaky and a bit sick.

Then I get out of bed, and strip off my shorts and T-shirt. I'll have a shower, and change my clothes, and phone Robert. The dream is still hanging around me, but I think it'll go when I'm with Robert and Kathy and Mikey and the others.

Chapter Eleven

A ND IT DOES.

Dad didn't mind me coming up to Robert's. We've all agreed that tomorrow, if it stays fine, we're going to go to the Open Air Leisure Centre, where there's a heated outdoor pool, and a jacuzzi, and rapids, and a wave machine, and lots of flumes. Paula wants to christen her bikini, and there's a baby-pool with inflatables for Sarah.

So tonight Dad's quite glad to have a quiet evening in. He's going to come and fetch me from Robert's at about half-past-ten, and then he'll have an early night. There's a programme he wants to watch. I wonder whether Paula will want to watch it too.

The dream vanishes like mist in the sun as soon as I step into Robert's kitchen. It's boiling with people. Even Johnny's there, the only one I haven't met before. He's just back from Scout camp, and Kathy's forcing him into the shower with a bottle of shampoo, and telling him she wants every stitch in the washing machine. Johnny's light and small, like Kathy. Somehow, looking at him, you can believe he plays the violin well. Mikey isn't in bed yet, and he's making the most of being up. He's eating mashed banana, plastering most of it over his face.

"Bad luck for us," says Robert. "We've to give him his bath."

Kathy's in a really good mood. She looks lit up, quite different from how she looked in the morning. They've had a great afternoon out, and now she and Robert's father are going for a Chinese meal, while Robert and I babysit.

"That's if you don't mind, Colette."

Stevie and Paul are still shovelling in spaghetti, but Kathy tells us we're not to touch the washing-up, it's Johnny's turn once he's out of the shower. They've left us some cans of shandy and a massive packet of crisps and a bottle of Coke for the kids.

Robert's dad comes in from getting ready. He's enormous, twice the size of Kathy. He doesn't look at all like my idea of a violinist. He has red hair and a red beard and the same light freckly skin as all the boys except Johnny. He blunders through the cauldron of children, looking for the iron so he can do his shirt. The iron's not in its right place and at last it's remembered that Robert took it into the boys' bedroom to iron some T-shirts for the little ones, and it's still there. Robert's father doesn't say a lot, but then he doesn't need to, since all the others talk all the time, and Kathy's got the radio on to catch the news as well. Then a friend of Johnny's appears at the back door. Apparently he's come to spend the evening too.

"That's nice," says Kathy. "You'll have a bit of company, Johnny." What can she mean? I look round and there seems to be company all over the house. The only problem would be trying to find somewhere to be alone.

"It's OK," says Robert to me, "they'll go off into our bedroom and play adventure games. You know the kind I mean. Johnny's mad about them."

Kathy and Mike leave, and we start scraping spaghetti and banana off Mikey before he goes in the bath. It's confusing, Robert's dad being called Mike as well. I suppose that's why they call the baby Mikey.

I've never bathed a baby before. Mikey can sit up on his own all right, but you have to watch him. He doesn't seem to know that you can't breathe underwater, and he keeps making dives for freedom while we soap him and wash his hair with baby shampoo. We have to wash his hair, because there's so much banana in it. Robert says you have to do it most days. Robert puts Mikey's nappy on, because I haven't got a clue. Then he goes off to fetch a sleeping-suit, while I hold Mikey.

Mikey smells lovely. He's getting sleepy, and he nestles up against me. The first time I've seen him not jumping about. He moans a bit while Robert puts him into the sleeping-suit, then Robert gets his bottle and I give it to him. It's gone in no time. Mikey vacuums it down, then his eyes start rolling up in his head as if he's drunk, and we lower him over the cot-bars, pull his quilt over him, and tiptoe out. He lets out a roar, but it's just a token protest, as Robert says. In a couple of minutes, he's asleep.

The little ones don't have to go to bed yet. We hand out Coke and crisps and they watch cartoons on the video while Robert and I drink coffee in the kitchen. I don't feel like shandy. Robert drinks a can of lager, then has coffee too. Johnny's done the washing-up and disappeared with his friend, and the kitchen's bare, tidy and quiet. You can hear the fridge hum.

I tell Robert about Paula and we get talking about

going abroad and really travelling. I even tell him about the travel competition, and we try to think of ways I could get round not having been anywhere. But we don't come up with any.

"I could write it, I know I could," I say, "it's just I haven't got the material."

"You could make it up," suggests Robert. "Talk to Paula. She'd give you the material and then you could make it sound as if you'd been there."

"No, it wouldn't work. It's a travel-writing competition. You need the experience. And then, if I did win, they'd ask questions about it and they'd find out it was all lies. It'd be really embarrassing."

"You could always write about Weston."

"What on earth would I write about Weston? *I went to the beach, I swam in the sea, I ate an ice-cream.* That'd be really great, wouldn't it?"

"Travelling isn't just about places, though, is it? It's about people, too. The people you meet."

I don't take this in at the time, because I am thinking about Turkey and Switzerland and the Ukraine. But later on, it comes back to me.

It's the people you meet.

Later on we listen to tapes and shift the kids off to bed. I try to get Robert to play something on his violin, but he won't. I think it's because Johnny's in the house. I think he would otherwise.

"I'll get Johnny to play for you when he comes down," says Robert. "He'll play for you."

After this, we both go quiet. I keep wondering if Robert's going to touch me, or try to kiss me. But he doesn't. Lots of boys would have made a move, when I had Mikey on my lap and Robert was putting on his sleeping-suit, but Robert didn't. I'm sure he likes me, though.

I'm glad really that we can just sit like this, listening to music and talking when we feel like it, with the kids asleep upstairs. I still feel jagged and churned up inside, because of the dream. And because of Caz. I don't think that I'm thinking of Caz, but every so often his face comes to me, looking as it looked when he was talking to me about caving. Warm, alive. Concentrating on me.

But I'm kidding myself. He can't be interested in me. He's sixteen, and he looks eighteen. I'm only thirteen.

I sigh, much more deeply than I mean to, and Robert looks at me.

"Are you tired, Colette? Do you want to go home?"

"No, I'm OK. I had a sleep earlier. But I had a horrible dream . . ." I tail off. I realise I don't want to talk about it, because it might bring it all back.

"Colette," says Robert.

"Mmm? What?"

"Don't go."

"What do you mean?" I ask.

But I know. And I know that Caz has been in Robert's mind all evening, just as much as he's been in mine.

"You know. Don't go caving with Caz."

"He said he'd take me somewhere easy."

"Caz's idea of easy wouldn't be the same as yours. I mean it. You don't know Caz like I do. He doesn't know where to stop."

"He seemed all right today. We had a nice time, didn't we?"

This time it's Robert who sighs, impatiently.

"Can't you see what he's like? No, I suppose you can't.

He takes a bit of getting to know, does Caz. But I wish you'd take my word for it."

"But what do you mean? He wouldn't try to hurt me, would he?"

Robert is quiet for a moment, then he says, "No, not really. Not if you put it like that. He wouldn't mean to do anything dangerous. Or if he did, it'd be in a part of him he doesn't want to know about."

I give up. This is getting too complicated for me, and I'm sure that Robert is exaggerating. "I'll be all right. I won't go anywhere dangerous, even if he does want to."

"Have you ever been in a cave, Colette?"

"Well, no, not really. I only want to just go in. I'm going to stay near the entrance, whatever Caz does."

"As long as you do. You mustn't think you can go anywhere Caz goes. He's an experienced caver."

"Then he won't take risks, will he? They don't, experienced people, do they?"

"No, they don't," says Robert in a defeated voice. "But I wish I could make you understand. I'm not getting it across."

"I'll make us another coffee," I say. But as I'm getting up, a thought strikes me. "Robert. Don't you say anything to my dad."

"No of course not, why should I?" he answers, so quickly that I'm sure he's been thinking of doing just that.

"Or to Kathy. Promise. You've got to promise."

"OK, OK!" says Robert, shielding his face as if fending off gunfire, and there's a chance to make a joke of the whole thing. I seize it. It's not really serious. It's not going to happen, and if it does it'll be all right and afterwards we'll wonder what all the fuss was about.

Won't we?

Chapter Twelve

IT'S HALF-PAST-eleven by the time I get back from Robert's. Dad arrives to drive me back just as Kathy and Mike get home, and they ask him in for a drink. I've never seen Dad like this, so relaxed and so outgoing with people. Or perhaps it's just that I don't often see him with other people, sitting over a drink and having a good time? Because I don't go to Birmingham very often, I know he always keeps the time free for me, and so we spend a lot of time on our own together, going out and visiting places and having special meals he's cooked and all that stuff. It's nice, but it's very intense. At the end of the week or however long it is, I'm quite glad to be in a train carriage where nobody knows me and nobody's looking at me when they don't think I'm noticing, to check whether I'm having a good time or not.

We stumble into the dark chalet, and although it's so late, Dad starts switching on lights and asking me if I'm hungry. I am quite, because we had our tea early, so he says he'll make us some toast and hot chocolate, and we go into the kitchen.

The kitchen looks nice at night. Nicer than it does in

the daytime, when its smallness makes it feel poky. At night, it looks like the cabin of a boat, because of the wooden walls and the shape of the windows and the way everything's handy and miniature. Dad whistles as he makes the chocolate. There isn't a blender, so he whisks it up with a hand-whisk, and grates some block chocolate on top. I make the toast, and spread honey on it.

"Seems ages since we got here, doesn't it?" says Dad.

I nod, because my mouth's full of toast.

We eat and drink. It's very peaceful in the kitchen, but I don't feel sleepy. I feel as if I could go for a ten-mile walk, or stay up all night talking.

"I thought it'd be nice to go out to a country pub for lunch tomorrow," says Dad.

"With Paula and Diane?"

"Yes, would you like that?"

Quick glance that I'm not supposed to notice. I know what to say.

"Mmm, yeah, that's fine."

"Only it's not much of a holiday for them, without a car. Not going anywhere."

"No."

"It can't be good for a marriage, when one partner goes off and works abroad like that," Dad continues.

"I suppose they must need the money. Dave earns loads in Saudi. Diane said."

"Yes, but it's not worth it, is it? He hasn't seen that baby since she was two weeks old. You don't think, that's the trouble, not when you're young. You think everything'll be all right, no matter what you do. You don't realise how quickly people change. How much they change."

He's not talking about Diane and her husband any

more. He's talking about Mum. About Mum and him, and what happened to them.

"You just don't realise," Dad repeats. "I should have seen, with someone like your mother, that she wouldn't be happy staying at home on her own. I mean, she'd always worked and we'd gone out almost every night, and then suddenly we had you and everything changed. I thought she'd like being at home with the baby. I was working all the hours God sends, trying to get promotion at school, and she was going mad at home with you. We had no money. She didn't even have a washing-machine. And then when she did go back to work, I told her it was wrong to leave you with a childminder. That was Tina, you won't remember her. I didn't know how bad it was all making her feel. If only we'd sat down and talked about it then, maybe we could have worked it out. But perhaps you always think that. The trouble is, you drift apart. You each have your own life. Then suddenly you turn round and there's no real reason for you to be together any more."

Dad's wrong. I do remember Tina. I remember sitting in the big dark green double pushchair and Tina fastening the plastic flap under my chin. I remember Tina saying, "*Arms up, knees stretch!*" when she peeled off my T-shirt. I don't know how old I was, though.

Dad's never talked about any of this before. He's talked about Mum, of course, and about how I mustn't feel any of it was my fault, and how they'll both always love me and all the rest of it. But not about how he felt himself.

I wonder if Diane's starting to feel like this about Dave? Maybe she does.

Dad smiles, and puts his hand over mine for a moment.

"I shouldn't be telling you all this, Colette. You mustn't let it worry you. Anyway, it's all in the past now."

Is it? Can anything like that be in the past? When I'm here, reminding each one of them of the other one?

When you frown like that, you look just like your father.

Don't leave your stuff lying about all over the floor like that! Why can't you put things away, like I do?

I wish I had curly hair like you, Mum.

Oh, I know everything's wonderful at Dad's!

"Your little girl's got your smile, hasn't she?" (A woman in a café said this to Mum's boyfriend, Steve, when he was out with Mum and me one Saturday.)

Does your mother allow you to do that, Colette?

"You're having a good time yourself, Colette? Enjoying the holiday."

Good old Dad. He can never resist asking.

"Yes. Of course I am. It's brilliant."

"Robert seems a nice boy."

You wish. Hope on, Dad. Why is it that the boys your parents think are nice are never the ones who make you melt inside when they look at you?

"Yes, he is. He's really nice. Dad, what are you thinking of for tomorrow? Apart from the pub lunch."

"Oh well, I thought maybe we'd just take it easy. Go on the beach if it's sunny. What are your plans?"

What are my plans? This is a giant step for mankind! A holiday with Dad in which every minute hasn't been arranged by him so that I won't get bored or lonely or want to go back to London. This is the breakthrough I've been working towards since I was eleven and stopped thinking it was terrific to have Dad to myself all day long. And the stupid thing is, I actually haven't got any plans for tomorrow. Robert said, "See you tomorrow," when I left with Dad, but we didn't arrange anything.

Tomorrow's Friday. Only one more day left till Saturday.

Dad carries on: "I know you're getting to the age when you don't want to be with me all the time. I was having a word with Diane . . ."

Oh, so Diane's behind this change of approach? I'm grateful to her, but I wonder why she has succeeded where I've always failed.

". . . so as long as I know what you're doing and what time you're going to be back . . ."

Oh Dad, you've still got a lot to learn, if you think that any parents ever really know what their kids are doing. But it's a good try.

". . . I know I can trust you. You've got your head screwed on."

All this is making me feel so guilty that I go round behind Dad's chair and hug him. Any minute now I'll blab about Caz and caving. But I don't. Instead I say, "Thanks, Dad. I wouldn't do anything stupid, you know that."

"It's just there are so many dangers, at your age. Especially in London. I suppose Mum's talked to you about – "

"Oh yes," I say quickly, embarrassed, "Mum's always talking to me about drugs and AIDS and getting pregnant."

"Oh. Well. That's all right then. As long as you know. I mean of course it's all a long way off, but it's best to know about all these things."

"Yes, Dad."

A long way off. I think of Claudia. Really, now, I'm glad that Mum wouldn't let me do what Claudia does.

Dad trusts me. I won't go off caving with Caz. In a

93

van he hasn't got a licence to drive. To a place I don't know. With someone I hadn't even met this time last week. Who's three years older than me, and looks five years older. Who *doesn't know when to stop*.

No, I won't go caving with Caz.

This is what I think, at 11.59 on Thursday evening.

At 10.27 on Friday morning, I'm flat out on the beach, sunbathing. It's another boiling hot day, and I'm quite glad we're going off into the country later, where it'll be cool and green. I am wearing my yellow bikini, which makes my stomach and legs look even browner than they are, and my skin glistens with sun-oil. Diane's done my hair again, plaiting thin yellow ribbons into it this time. I wouldn't wear it like this at home, but it looks fine for the beach. Di's coming down to sunbathe for half an hour, before we go out, but she's not bringing Sarah. The beach is too hot for Sarah today, and Paula's taken her off for a walk round the lanes that stretch back from Kewstoke, with a big white canopy over her buggy. I'm sleepy, because by the time I got to bed last night it was half-past-twelve, and I still had that lit-up feeling which always keeps me awake, even when I'm tired out. But I didn't have any dreams.

I shut my eyes, and red sun patterns dance behind my lids. The heat soaks into my body, and I drift, listening to children's voices and the birds singing back in the woods.

Something cold and wet lands on my stomach and I shoot up, blinking. My eyes take a minute to adjust to the glare, then I see that it's Caz, standing over me like a dark pillar, and that it's sea-water dripping onto my stomach. He's got something in his hand, twisting like an electric cable. I back away from him. Gritty sand rubs into my thighs.

94

"What's that? What're you doing?"

In one easy movement Caz folds himself up and kneels down on the sand next to me. The flapping thing in his hand comes near to my face.

"Urrgh! Get it away! It's horrible! What is it?"

"Don't you eat eels in London! Course you do! Eel pie, I've read about it. This is a little'un though, you oon't get eel pie off 'ee."

"Don't talk like that," I say crossly.

"Loike wha? We ent Lunnun folk yer," says Caz, bringing the eel back into my field of vision.

It isn't flapping. It's whipping about like a piece of loose electric cable after a hurricane. It has a black blunt head, a bit wider than its body, and I'm sure I can see teeth as the head slashes about. I shudder and back off some more.

"Where'd you get it?"

"Caught it in a rock pool."

"Put it back in a rock pool! I don't want it near me!"

For answer, Caz stands up, whirls the eel around his head like a cowboy's lassoo rope, then lets go. The eel flies about fifty yards through the air, and lands in the mud.

"That's horrible, Caz! Why didn't you put it back in the water?"

Caz sits down again. "What're you bothered about? You didn't like it, did you? You told me to get rid of it."

"Yes, but it was alive. Why kill it, just for nothing?"

"You a vegetarian, or something?"

"No."

"Well, then. What do you think happens in abattoirs? What do you think happens on fishing-boats? You ever seen a catch of mackerel flapping about on the quay? They

95

take a long time to die, some of them. But you eat them, don't you? Why get upset about an eel."

Put like that, it does sound as if Caz is right and I'm wrong. But all the same, I know he isn't.

Caz picks up my Bruce Chatwin and studies the cover. "It's a good book, isn't it?" he says. "Have you read THE SONGLINES?"

I stare at him. Even though Robert keeps saying how clever Caz is, I haven't thought of him as someone who'd read much. There's a little smile in the corners of Caz's mouth, and I am sure he knows what I'm thinking.

"I can see you've got a lot of wrong ideas about me," says Caz, "I wonder what Robert's been telling you?"

"He hasn't been telling me anything," I lie automatically.

"That's good. You can find out for yourself."

He lies down beside me, and shuts his eyes. I lie back myself, and close mine, and drink in the sun again. It's the first time I've felt relaxed with Caz. We lie there for ages. I don't know how long. I'm just falling asleep again when I feel another touch. But this time it's warm. Caz is running his finger very gently round the curve of my forehead, round my cheek, stroking the shape of my face. It feels so lovely. I keep very still, my eyes shut, pretending I'm asleep. After a minute, he stops.

"Colette?"

"Mmm?"

"You looking forward to Saturday?"

"Yes."

Then Diane arrives, with her big blue beach-towel and a bottle of Perrier. Caz doesn't stay.

It's 11.24.

I'm going caving with Caz tomorrow.

Chapter Thirteen

WHEN WE WERE little kids, we used to play Grandmother's Footsteps in the school playground. If you were Grandmother, you had to go and stand with your face turned towards the trunk of a tree which grew in between the railings. It was the only tree in the school, and lots of kids cut their initials into it, though we weren't allowed to. I don't remember what kind of tree it was. Not a conker tree or anything special like that. It had bark which you could peel off in long strips, and big leaves which we used to draw round in class sometimes.

You had to stand there with your face pressing against the bark. You weren't allowed to look round. And there wouldn't be a sound behind you as the other kids began to creep very very slowly from the starting line. Then you'd know they were coming nearer because there'd be a whisper, or someone would snort through their nose trying not to laugh. But you couldn't tell how far away they were. The game was to let one of them get as near as you dared, then you could suddenly spring round and you'd have a good chance of catching them before they could get back to base. You had to take a risk. The closer they got, the more chance they had of catching you before you could turn round, then you'd be out. So you waited and waited, straining for the sound of footsteps, ready to whirl round, listening. And then sometimes you got it wrong and there wasn't any time left and you just heard a rush of breath and a shriek before someone jumped on you.

I can see that tree-trunk now. Every detail of it. The colour, dark, and then light where the bark had peeled. The big gouge where someone'd been carving it with a penknife. KATIE 4 – but a teacher must have come along, because the other name was missing. Everything clear and sharp, like the last thing you see before you die.

Everyone wanted to be Grandmother, but once you were there, all on your own with all your friends on the starting line giggling together and looking at you, you wished you were back with them.

When something's going to happen to me, something important, I still get the same feeling as I used to get when I had to stand against that tree and not look round. Something's creeping up on you, and you want to play, but at the same time your heart starts to thump in your chest and your hands go sticky and you know if you had to say anything your voice would wobble. It was like that when I started at Mary Fisher. That's our secondary school. The night before our first day, Angelina and I must have phoned each other about eight times.

Listen, don't be late! You get into really bad trouble at Mary Fisher if you're late.

What if the Tube's delayed?

What if someone jumps on the line and they stop the trains?

Have you got change ready so we can use the auto-matic ticket machines?

D'you feel scared?

Yeah! Really scared!

Me, too.

Hey, remember your lunch money. If you don't have it, you don't eat.

Then after about two days there we felt as if we'd always been meeting up at the corner by the High Street and walking down to the Tube and making sure we stood in the right place so we could get on first and maybe get a seat.

There's nobody to talk to about this, though. Nobody to phone eight times. I did think about calling Angelina, but it would take so long to tell her the whole story. Besides, I know what she'd say. She'd tell me not to go.

I've talked to Robert again. He isn't happy about it, but he agrees that I can tell Dad I'm spending the morning with him and Caz, and he'll be up at the stables anyway, so Dad isn't likely to see him. I tell Dad that I'm going up to the stables on Saturday morning, then maybe out with Caz and Robert. I'll be back soon after one.

Caz left a message for me at Robert's. He'll pick me up from the chalet, but not in the van. The van'll be parked about a quarter of a mile down the road. I wonder how Caz dares to drive the van in the village, where everyone must know how old he is. Robert says they turn a blind eye. I didn't know this, but he says Caz's dad lost his licence for a year because of drink-driving. So people don't say anything when they see Caz in the van. Besides, Caz is careful. He doesn't drive through towns if he can help it.

I've thought about it so many times. Caz coming

through the gate and knocking on the kitchen door. Me going out to meet him. Saying goodbye to Dad. Walking down our path side by side. No, it's too narrow. OK, one after the other. It doesn't sound quite as good, but never mind. Then down the lane to Caz's van.

I think about it over and over. It's coming nearer and nearer. It's catching up with me.

Chapter Fourteen

I'M LIVING THROUGH a film I've already watched six times. Or a film that's having to be shot again and again because it's never quite right.

Take one. CAZ ARRIVES AT THE BYRNE CHALET.

Dad's making some French toast, and he's overheated the frying pan so the kitchen stinks of hot fat. I've told him I don't want anything to eat, but he's still begging me to try his toast and telling me how delicious it is when Caz knocks on the door.

Dad opens it, frying-pan in hand like a weapon. He frowns at Caz as if he doesn't know who he is, though I've told him twice that morning and once the night before, speaking clearly and distinctly so that there's absolutely no chance he'll come out with, '*I didn't know anything about this, Colette*' in front of Caz.

But once Dad gets his brain into gear he puts down the frying-pan and becomes quite talkative, though in a way which I know means he doesn't much like the look of Caz. He says how much he appreciates Robert giving me lessons, and that he expects Caz'll want to go off on his own because he wouldn't want to be stuck with a beginner. Caz doesn't say a lot, but it's all OK. There's nothing Dad could object to. Nothing to make him leap to the doorway and bar our exit with a flaming frying-pan.

I say goodbye to Dad, and suddenly I've got to get out of this kitchen because I can't cope with all the love and trust in Dad's face and the way he just takes it for granted that everything I tell him is true, and the way he says, "Have a good time, see you later," as if it's an ordinary morning and just a matter of the clock going round a few times before he sees me again. It feels, for once, as if we really live together, all the time.

The air outside feels clear and cool and open after the heat in the kitchen. It's not such a nice day, and the clouds are moving fast. I've worn Johnny's jeans again, and a tracksuit top and my heavy shoes. I've got a much thicker sweater in my carrier bag. The sweater's one Mum knitted me. And I've got a waterproof jacket. Robert said I'd need it.

Caz walks ahead of me. He's dressed just as usual, but he says his stuff's in the van, and when we get to it I see the yellow helmets with lights in them and the other equipment in the back. Ropes.

Surely we won't need ropes? I expect he keeps the stuff in the back of the van all the time. After all, he goes caving regularly.

"I got you a helmet," says Caz. "Should fit. Haven't you got boots?"

"No."

"Let's see the grips on those."

I turn my foot over and show Caz the ridged soles of my heavy shoes.

"Could be worse," he says.

He's very quiet. I can't work out whether he's friendly or not today. It's as if he's wiped out the way we lay side by side on the beach, and he stroked my face. Can people wipe out things like that so easily? I can't.

I climb into the van's front passenger seat and fasten my seat-belt. The van smells of metal and oil. There are lots of fag-ends in the ashtray, too, and more rope by my feet. Caz backs the van out, and onto the road.

"Hold tight," he says, and I do. This is just as well. Caz is hard on the van, and in return it's hard on us. We jounce around inside its bare metal shell like rice in a tin. Or at least, I do. Caz is a lot heavier than me, and he's used to it.

He pulls the van up with a jerk by the village shop, and the door slams, then slowly opens again. I sit there perched up on the seat, out of breath and not sure whether I'm going to last out the van ride without being sick. In a minute Caz comes out of the shop with another man. They stand on the doorstep with the wind blowing their hair back. The man's big and greasy, with his jeans slipping down over his backside. He laughs at something Caz says, and for a moment I'm afraid that he's going to climb in the van with us. But he doesn't. He raises a hand, and rolls off, hitching his trousers.

Caz dumps two big bars of chocolate on my lap, and some shortbread with a thistle on it.

"You'll need that later," he says.

I wonder if he can guess that I've been too wound up to eat breakfast.

The rest of the journey is as bad as the beginning. I don't look where we're going. I don't dare. I clutch the bar fixed to the roof on my left side, and hold on as we bucket down country lanes, and pray that we won't meet any cows or tractors or people like Paula pushing baby-buggies. Long green grass whips the sides of the van, and white flower-heads fly in through the window. I have to keep the window open, even though the wind is tugging my hair out of its plait, or else I *will* be sick. I don't look at Caz. I really do not want to know what kind of look he has on his face. Or whether he is enjoying this. I shut my eyes and count the minutes.

Just as suddenly as before, Caz jams on the brakes. The chocolate shoots off my lap, and the seat-belt cuts into my stomach, but I'm past caring. We've stopped. In the silence, I hear birds sing. We're right up against a hedge.

"There's a gate just behind us, Colette. Can you get out and open it?"

My fingers feel dimly for the seat-belt catch, then for the door handle. I step down onto solid, red earth, churned up by tractor tyres then dried into deep ruts. I smell a fresh green smell made up of hedges and crushed grass and flowers whose names I don't know.

I stagger to the gate and untie the thick orange twine round the gate-post. The gate swings open quite easily, and I stand by it while Caz starts the engine again and reverses the van in through the gate. It jolts over the ruts, and I'm glad I'm not still in it. Caz keeps on backing it until it's right alongside the hedge, and hidden from the road. He cuts the engine again, and jumps out, holding the chocolate and the shortbread.

I stand in a daze, pulling up long threads of grass and sucking their juicy ends. I don't want to go anywhere or do anything. It's enough to be out of the van, in the silence, smelling the fields. But Caz has other ideas. He opens the van's back doors and starts unloading gear, and reluctantly I go across, feeling I ought to help. He gets out an old-fashioned battered metal flask and asks, "You want coffee?"

I say yes, and he pours me some. I'm amazed that the inside of the flask hasn't smashed to pieces, but it seems all right. No slivers of glass or anything. It's too strong for me though, and I hand the cup back to Caz, half-full.

"You'll get thirsty down there," he warns me.

"I'm fine. I'll have some later."

Down there. I look across the fields, but I can't see any caves, or anywhere that looks like a place there might be caves. Everything's flat and calm.

But I don't ask Caz. Once I've asked, he'll tell me, and then we'll have to go.

"See that clump of trees over there?" says Caz. "That's where we're going."

"What's in there? Is the cave there?"

"There's a swallet."

"What's that?"

Caz points to a darker green wavering line that runs across the field.

"See that stream? It's all but dried up now, but you can see where it is. Where it goes underground, that's a swallet. Round here it's limestone, see. There's caves and caverns all underneath us."

I look down. I'm treading on eggshells, then. Underneath, it's all hollow. Is this what they mean when they say, *Keep your feet on the ground, Colette*?

"But we can't get down there. Not if there's a stream."

"Course we can. Easiest swallet in the south."

"But I thought, I mean I thought we were coming to look at a cave. You know. The sort you walk into. Where you can stand up and everything."

"Like at the seaside, you mean?"

Caz is smiling. He's more than smiling, he's laughing at me. He thinks I'm an idiot. And I am an idiot. Why didn't I find out? Why did I think that the real thing would be anything like the picture I'd got in my mind?

Swallet. What a word. Swallow. Swallow you up.

Ten. Nine. Eight. Seven. Six. Five. Four. Three. Two. One.

WE'RE COMING!

Chapter Fifteen

I'M SWEATING AS I pull on my heavy jersey and then my waterproof jacket. The sky is heavy with clouds now, and it feels thundery. Perhaps that's why my head aches.

"Here's your helmet," says Caz, and gives me the smaller of the two helmets. At first I think it isn't going to fit. It's much too big and it slips around on my head, even when I fix the straps. A rush of relief. Without a helmet, I can't go down.

"Come here," says Caz.

He lifts off the helmet, and twists up my hair around my head. With the thickness of my hair under it, the helmet stays in place and straps on firmly.

Caz puts a coil of rope over his shoulder.

"We won't need it," he tells me. "It's not steep this way down. But just in case."

We walk over the cool green field towards the trees. My feet feel as if they are walking on their own. I look down at them and they tread quite firmly. They know the way they're going and my fear hasn't reached them yet.

It's dark under the trees. There's a smell of stone, and

a trickle of water. The stream. We push between two tree-trunks and there it is. The entrance. A rough jumble of rock and mud and a dark place where the stream disappears.

Caz fixes his rope round a metal stake driven into a tree-trunk.

"You follow me," he says. "Turn round like this. I'll be in front of you, and I'll be telling you where to put your feet. I'll be able to see you, because you'll be against the light. You don't need to hold the rope, though. It's only there to guide you. You won't fall. Think of it like going down a steep hill, that's all it is."

I've never heard Caz talk like this. As if he understands what I'm afraid of and he's trying to put me at ease. *Like going down a steep hill.* I can manage that. I like climbing, and I don't mind heights.

Forget that the hill is under the earth. Don't think about where it goes down to.

Then with a quick sliding movement Caz ducks down and eases his body into the space where the muddy little stream disappears. I see his head, with his helmet light on. There's plenty of room. He's right, it's not a tight squeeze. Then he's gone.

I wait, standing under the trees. I feel more alone than I have ever felt in my life before.

Then Caz calls,

"Right! You can come on now Colette! Turn around, face the rock, and back down."

Am I going to go in? I don't want to. My stomach hurts and my legs have realised what's going on and they want to run. But I can't. I can't face the look of contempt on Caz's face. The way he'd slam the van door and drive back without speaking to me. Or would he even drive me back?

Stop it. You can't start thinking about people like that. Not if you're on your own with them, miles from anywhere.

No, it's way past the time for bursting into tears and asking to be taken home. If that was what I wanted I should have stayed on the beach eating ice-creams.

I walk over to the mouth of the swallet. It's the longest journey I've made in my life. I turn around, face the rock and get into position. It's not difficult. I can feel the angle of the rock and the stone going down. But not too steeply. Caz's right. The rock's damp, but not wet, because the stream's so low. I spread out, gripping the rock with my whole body, and go down slowly, like a crab, one step, another, then another . . .

"Good," says Caz's voice, below me but much closer than I'd thought. "Keep going like that. Keep to the right where it's dry."

I'm aware that the rock's bumping and scraping my knees through my jeans, but I don't feel it. All I feel is my foot, reaching down for the next grip, my hands letting go of the rock and then grasping it again. The rock's rougher than it looks, and there's a skin of dried mud on it which lodges under my nails.

I know I don't need to grip like this. I don't need to cling with my knees and hands and feet. I don't need to press myself tightly against the rock surface. It's only like going down a steep hill. But this time, I don't know what's at the bottom.

Or even where the bottom is.

There's still daylight coming through the gaps in the rock above me, but now the light from my helmet lamp is making sharp round patterns of light and darkness on the rocks. I'm not used to it. It seems to make the dark blacker, where it doesn't reach.

And the smell. I've never smelled anything like it before. A smell of dead things. Dead rocks, dead water, dead mud. Nothing green or juicy or alive. Dank, dark rock that the sun never touches.

I daren't look round to see Caz, but he keeps on talking to me. I've heard him talking like this before. When was it? I can't remember. Another step down, and another. Another foothold, another handhold.

It's not difficult.

"Come on now, a bit to your right, now let go that hand, you'll be fine, you don't need your hands here, come on now . . ."

I remember now. That's how Caz talks to horses.

And then my foot scrapes and doesn't go down any more, and there's Caz standing beside me. I let go of the rock, and stand up. My knees are trembling, but I'm down. The floor is flat and damp and wide, and the stream runs off, away to one side and out of sight. No, it doesn't run. It slithers away leaving a slimy trail like the trails you find after slugs have been crossing the pavements in the night.

Caz turns, and flashes his light. We're in a cave. A proper cave, wide and high and curving at the roof. There's a slightly different smell here, musty and a bit sharp. It smells like an old phone booth.

"You get too many tourists down here," says Caz, flashing his light round the walls. There's graffitti every-where: DIGGER WAS YER, BEDMIE BOYS RULE, SAVE THE WHALES . . .

"Youth club kids on a night out," says Caz contemptuously. "Cavers wouldn't do that. A real caver doesn't leave a trace of where he's been."

The way Caz says it, it sounds a bit sinister. A bit like someone wiping off fingerprints at the scene of the crime.

"What d'you reckon then, Colette?" Caz asks me. "You like it down here?"

"I don't know," I answer slowly. To my surprise, I'm telling Caz the truth. "It doesn't seem to me like somewhere human beings ought to be."

"All your ancestors lived in caves," Caz points out.

"They weren't like this though, were they? They had entrances."

"They've found cave-drawings hundreds of yards from the surface," says Caz. "Anyway, this is only a tourist cave. I'll show you something better than this."

And he goes across the cave to where there's a low channel in the rock, one I didn't even see when the light swept round the cave. There's so much darkness. In a way, our lights make it worse.

Caz crouches down in front of the hole.

"This one's more of a squeeze, but it's quite easy. It widens out after twenty metres. You'll see some good rock formations. The tourists don't come down here."

Caz is getting himself into position to enter the shallow channel headfirst through the rock, and he's still giving me instructions about following him and how there's one turn where I'll need to ease myself round slowly.

And I know that whatever happens, whatever it costs, I can't go down that hole into the darkness. There's a rushing sound in my ears. It's like when I'm in the Tube and I suddenly start thinking of all the houses on top of me, and the roads and the cars and the thick rock that lies between me and daylight and safety and freedom. The smell of rock chokes up my nose and mouth.

I can't breathe. My breath comes in short gasps. The air's bad. I've heard about that, about miners hitting bad air in the tunnels. I can't breathe. Sweat breaks out all over me and I hear a strange sound, like a whimper, coming out of my mouth.

I've got to get out. I've got to get out.

I look round frantically and my light bobs against smooth dark walls, making blodges of darkness everywhere. I can't see the way we came in.

It was that way. I turn and run and I crash into a wall of solid rock with a bruising thud. Blood's pounding in my ears but I hear Caz shout, "Colette" then I turn back again and I see him straighten up and come after me with a huge wavering shadow behind him, a shadow that grows and sways after me faster than I can run. Coming to take me away. Coming to swallow me up.

And I feel breath on the back of my neck and hundreds of hands reaching out to grab me.

We've got her! We've got her!

You're out, Colette!

You're out!

Out!

Out. Out. Out.

And just as I see a thread of grey light by one of the walls and lunge towards it, I feel a hand brush the back of my neck and I spin round, lose my footing on the slippery cave-floor, and crash down on the rock.

"Mum. Mum. Mum. Mm. Mm."

I'm still saying it over and over. I haven't fainted or anything. But I can't seem to stop crying. My back hurts.

"Jesus, Colette! What were you *doing*?"

It's Caz. He sounds furious. I press my lips together to stop the noises coming out.

"Colette! Colette!" Angry. And something else, too.

"My back. Hurt my back."

I can't move from where I've been slammed down on the rock. Something's sticking into my back, but that's not what hurts. It was when I twisted round while I was falling.

Caz is kneeling down and his light is shining into my face so I have to shut my eyes.

"Can you move your legs?"

I can. It hurts a lot, but my legs move. My feet flop apart.

"Can you sit up?"

I've forgotten what you have to do to sit up. I raise my head, but it makes me feel dizzy.

No. I can't sit up.

"What the hell did you run for?"

"You frightened me," I say. I seem to be getting into the habit of telling Caz the truth.

"I frightened you," repeats Caz. He sits back on his heels, looking at me. Then he gives me the strangest smile I've ever seen, and says, "Then you're not such a fool."

I don't answer. The pain in my back is hot and tearing. And my head hurts where I've banged it. My fingers are throbbing. I must have torn the skin against the rock.

What does he mean? *Then you're not such a fool.* Is that what Caz thought of me? That I was a fool who'd do anything to be with him.

It's true, though, isn't it. No getting away from it now, not while I'm lying on the cave floor with my back hurting so much I can't sit up.

And I'm with Caz all right. Very much so. My mind

takes this in, and begins to race in the way it does when it knows I need lots of help and there isn't much time to think.

Because I *am* afraid. Not of the cave any more. Not of the darkness. I think of the green fields above me, and I long for them with all my heart, but I'm not panicking any more. And my back's hurt, but I'm not afraid of that. I can't feel anything bleeding, and if you can move your legs, then it means you aren't paralysed. In a little while I'll be able to move.

But I'm afraid. Stories are drifting back into my mind, the kind of stories you try to forget, the kind of stories you shut your mind against. I'm getting more afraid every minute.

Of Caz.

Chapter Sixteen

I HAVE HEARD THAT animals can tell when you're afraid. They pick up a smell of fear from you, no matter how much you try to walk away slowly and calmly, no matter how much you say 'Good dog', no matter how casually you back towards the field-gate.

Caz is very close to me, leaning over me, leaning and looking. His face is in shadow. I can't see past the light. But I can see that his eyes are wide, and there's a shine on them that reminds me of the shine on the stream where it disappears into the darkness on the other side of the cave.

"Colette," he says.

His voice sounds funny, as if his throat is tight and dry, like mine.

"Yes," I say. To my surprise my voice comes out quite calm.

"You don't need to be frightened of me."

"I'm not frightened of you, Caz," I say lightly, carefully. "It was just for a moment, with the dark and the shadows. You didn't look like yourself."

"You needn't be frightened of me," he repeats, still in

that strange, tight voice that comes from a place I don't know. Maybe he doesn't know it either. It sounds like a voice coming out of a dream. "You're just a kid, aren't you?" he says. "You could be my kid sister."

"Yes," I say. "Yes, I could be your kid sister. I never had a brother. I'd have liked a brother."

Something seems to be telling me how to speak. Keep it calm, keep it light. Don't cry. Don't let him see you're frightened.

"I never had a sister," says Caz. "My mum had her insides taken away. But it didn't do her any good. The cancer had spread, see. The last time I saw her, she was all yellow. The cancer had got to her liver."

Keep quiet. Don't say anything. Let him talk.

And in the dark, silent cave, Caz's voice goes on and on. He doesn't touch me, but he leans so close I can feel his breath on my face. I can smell the coffee we drank up there, in the daylight world.

"She had long hair," says Caz. "But it all fell out when she got ill. Dad wanted her to get a wig, but she wouldn't. It grew back in little curls. I used to put my finger in one of her curls. I thought if her hair was growing back, she must be all right."

I feel Caz's hand, touching my hair.

"Same colour as yours," says Caz. "But they say your toenails go on growing, don't they? Even when you're dead. Even when you're shut away under ground. They put a lining round her grave. Green grass. Plastic greengrocer's grass. But I wasn't such a fool as they thought. I smelled the earth underneath. You can smell it if you want."

There's someone in this cave I've never seen, never known. The Caz I know has gone.

"Told her to get a wig," says Caz. "Bastard."

I feel his hand tremble at the back of my neck, touching my skin.

"It's nice here," says Caz, stroking my hair.

I lie very still. As long as I keep reminding him of a sister, he won't hurt me. Because I know for sure now what I've known since the first moment I saw Caz. What I've hidden from myself. What Robert knows too, and tried to tell me.

That Caz very much wants to hurt someone.

That Caz very much needs to hurt someone.

That Caz is someone who *never knows when to stop.*

Angelina, I swear to God, if I get out of this I'll go to all those self-defence classes you've been trying to get me enrolled in.

"Bastard," says Caz again, and his hand tightens on my hair. I move a little and the pain in my back burns. The pain steadies me. Without it, I know I'd scream.

"Caz," I say, very casually, very quietly. "I like this cave. I'm glad you showed it to me. We'll have to come caving again. You can teach me. Like I was your sister."

"You wouldn't come with me. I wanted you to stay with me, but you wouldn't. You let me go on my own."

Who's he talking to? He's talking to someone and it's not me. I must think, I must think. Who's he talking to?

"Caz. Caz. I want to come with you. But I can't. You can help me, Caz. You can make me better."

Slowly, reluctantly, his hands leave my hair. He moves back a little way.

"We could stay here. It's nice here," he says. "Don't you want to stay with me?"

"I'm going to stay. I won't move. I'll always be here.

But I need you to help me. I need you to go and get help for me."

There's a long silence. I can feel Caz's eyes on me, but I don't look at him. I lie and feel the rock under me, and I watch the faint grey trace of daylight coming down from the field. Nothing matters any more except that little streak of grey. I feel cool and empty. I can't fight Caz any longer. I can't find a voice to answer him with any more.

Slowly and awkwardly, Caz gets up. I've never seen him move awkwardly like this before. He takes off his waterproof jacket, and his thick sweater. My body tenses, prickling all over. Then he folds the sweater, carefully and neatly, like someone doing it the way he's been taught. He bends down, lifts my head, and slips the sweater under it, like a pillow. Then he spreads his waterproof coat over me and tucks it in at the sides.

"That'll keep you warm," he says. "In case I'm gone a long time."

And quickly and lightly he crosses the cave and shimmies up the side of the rock. The grey stain of daylight vanishes as his body blocks the shaft. I hear a clatter of small stones, then a couple of minutes later the trace of daylight is back on the wall. He's gone. It's all so quick. He doesn't stop, or call back to me.

I strain my ears, but I can't hear the van drive off. Would I hear it, right down here? I don't know. Probably not.

And I'm alone in the cave. There are sounds I didn't hear before. At first I was too frightened, then I was concentrating on Caz's voice. I blocked out everything from my mind but Caz's voice. Now I hear the slight trickle from the stream, and water dripping off a rock at the back of the cave. It's not a regular sound. One tock, then a pause, another tock. It's got all the time in the world.

And I won't be afraid. I've been afraid for so long I've used up all my fear. And my back's hurting more and more. You can't think of anything else once the pain starts. I don't mind. You can't think of anything else.

I'm cold and sleepy and my back hurts, but I'm not afraid. And yet I'm underground. And on my own. My friends wouldn't believe how calm I feel. They know what I'm like in the Tube when it stops in a tunnel.

Cold comes up through the rock. The coat and the sweater help, but not much. I'm very tired. I've switched off my helmet light. I don't know how long they last. I didn't bother to find out anything like that, when I had the chance. I didn't even drink any of the coffee.

Drop by drop, the water moves down the rock-face. Tock. Tock. I lie and watch the light on the wall.

Chapter Seventeen

DAMAGE TO THE SACRO-ILIAC JOINT. That's way down in my back, where the pain is. *Shock and exposure, extensive bruising, cuts to the head.*

I was wrong about there not being any blood. There was, but it was all at the back of my head, so I didn't feel it. It must have soaked into Caz's sweater. I don't know what happened to his sweater, or his waterproof coat.

The nurses had to cut off some of my hair so they could stitch the cut. I don't know how much hair has gone. It's hard to believe, but I don't really care. I might even get all my hair cut, properly. Then I'll get my ears pierced, because people will be able to see the ear-rings.

I got the doctor to tell me what was wrong with me in real words. I was tired of people saying things like,

We'll just pop you up on this bed.

Just one more little injection, Colette.

Don't worry about anything, dear. Just go back to sleep.

I've been very lucky, the doctor says. My back will be fine, it's just a matter of time. It'll be painful for six weeks or so. A few days ago I'd have screamed "SIX WEEKS!" as if I'd been sentenced to death, but not now.

When I woke up in the cave, everything was the same. I thought I was still dreaming, and I tried to wake up, but the cold under me wouldn't go away. I was still alone. The smudge of grey light was there, the cold was there, the trickle of the stream was there. And so was the pain in my back and in my head, only much worse now. I put my helmet light on, but I still couldn't see properly. And I was so thirsty. In my pocket I had some of the chocolate Caz had bought but I couldn't eat it. I felt too sick and dizzy. I looked at my watch and it was only quarter to one. Dad wouldn't even be expecting me back yet. It would be an hour, maybe two hours, before he began to miss me. Before he began to get worried. And I'd made Robert promise not to say where I'd gone. I tried to turn round and get more comfortable, but it hurt too much. I must have gone back to sleep again.

It went on like that. Sleeping a bit, then waking up and thinking hours must have passed. Looking at my watch and finding it was only ten minutes since I'd looked at it last. Dreaming I was looking at my watch. Hearing the water, and smelling the stone. Getting colder and drowsier. Sleeping again.

It was quarter to three when the Cave Rescue people came. I know that, because they told me in the ambulance. But by then I wasn't looking at my watch any longer, because my arm felt so heavy when I tried to lift it. I wasn't really asleep, but I don't remember things clearly, in the way you remember things that happen in normal life. I remember it in the way you remember dreams. I can't remember hearing them coming. Then the cave was full of big men in bright waterproof jackets. There were voices and lights and people moving all around me, and I started to shake because it was a shock after the dark and the quiet which seemed to have been going on for ever. I remember someone asked me if I could move my legs. Then I was strapped onto a stretcher, then I don't remember much until I felt daylight on my face. It was blinding, even though I don't think the sun was shining. I shut my eyes because the light was making them water, and one of the men thought I was crying. He gave me a tissue, and I told him I was all right.

When I was in the ambulance someone said to me, "Don't worry, you'll soon be fancying a cheese-and-pickle sandwich again."

I was going to say I didn't like pickle, but I don't think I did. I must have fallen asleep again. Then after a bit Dad was there. I don't know when he arrived. It might have been when I'd got to hospital. He was wearing his waterproof jacket and there was water shining on it, so it must have been raining. His hair was wet and his face was an awful colour. He looked terrible. When he saw me I thought he was going to cry, but he didn't. He held my hand and said they'd soon have me all cleaned up, so I thought I must look pretty bad. I started telling him it was OK, I wasn't paralysed because I could move my legs, then I think he did cry.

I've slept more or less since then, apart from when the doctor came in to see me just now. They've put me in what's called an observation cubicle, but I'll be moving onto a ward today, because I haven't got concussion. I know I've had a head x-ray and a back x-ray, but I can't remember much about them. I had to move my legs about a lot, and focus on lights and things like that. The doctor says Dad's coming in later. He was here most of the night, but then he went home to get a few hours' sleep. Back to the chalet, I mean.

There's a fold of white sheet on my chest, and a white locker beside my bed. I can hear a Hoover going down the ward, and a cleaner banging lockers. I never thought I'd be so glad to hear a Hoover. I can turn my head a bit without it hurting too much, and out of the window I've been watching two little brown birds pecking away at crumbs somebody's thrown out. They're sparrows, I think. Now they're fighting over the last few crumbs. And I can hear two nurses talking at the nursing station. One of them's telling the other about a film she went to last night. It sounds good. But the other one says she doesn't fancy that sort of film, she thinks there's much too much sex in the cinema these days. Then a buzzer goes and they stop talking, and I hear footsteps going away down the corridor. I can smell the hospital smell of clean sheets and disinfectant and a faint hidden smell of sickness and bloody dressings. It feels so safe here.

I stretch as much as I can, and look at the green cotton bedspread sticking up where my feet are. There's a smell of coffee. They must be bringing drinks round. I feel as if I've been rescued from a shipwreck, after hours of floating in cold green water, clinging on to a spar of wood that keeps going down under my weight. Now I'm warm and wrapped up in blankets and safe in the captain's cabin.

But I wonder if the people who were rescued from the Titanic ever got the feeling of cold and ice and desperation out of their bones. I wonder if I'll forget the dead smell of the cave, and the cold coming up from the rock.

The glass door opens. I turn my head, and see Robert coming towards my bed, looking exactly the same as usual. Hair that won't quite lie down. Freckles and battered jeans. But no grin.

He stands by the bed. He's nervous. Neither of us know what to say. This is worse than the first time we met.

"Hi Robert," I croak. I clear my throat and try again. Maybe it's the damp of the cave that's got into my throat.

"You all right, Colette?" he asks nervously. He pinches a fold of the sheet between his fingers and stares down at me. How different it feels from Caz's stare. Suddenly it's Caz I can see there. Caz sitting beside me, so close I can feel the heat of his body. Caz going on and on in that tight, monotonous voice. Caz's eyes, so dark you can't see the pupil.

"Yeah, I'm OK," I say.

Now my voice is trembling. This is stupid! You know how not to cry when you don't want to, I tell myself fiercely. I pinch my left earlobe hard, and the tears go back down inside my eyes.

"You look awful," says Robert. "What've you done to your face?"

"It's just bruising and cuts. Contusions, I mean," I say, remembering the medical terminology. "And a few scrapes here and there. It won't leave any scars, except under my hair."

"What happened?" asks Robert.

"I fell. I was running. In the cave. And I fell."

I don't want to say any more, and luckily Robert sees it and changes the subject.

"Your parents are downstairs," he says. "They're having a coffee. They said I could come up first. Your mum's a bit upset so I think she wants to calm down before she sees you."

"My *parents*! You mean Mum's here? What's she doing?"

"What do you think she's doing? You disappear. We all freak out. As soon as he knew what happened, and that you were OK, your dad phoned her. He was going to phone her before, but my mum thought he should wait because it would be so awful for her, being up in London. It would take her ages to get here. And thinking what might have happened to you all the way. But then she was out, and your dad couldn't get through to her till nine in the evening. She got the train straight down, but it was too late to come and see you last night."

"Where did she sleep?"

"At the chalet, I suppose."

"Wow," I say slowly and thoughtfully.

I lie and think about it. Mum and Dad in the chalet. Together. I can't remember them being together since the awful changeovers when I was a little kid. Both of them polite, both of them tense when they kissed me. One saying hello to me, one saying goodbye. It always had to be like that.

I look at Robert.

"Your hair's soaking," I say. "Is it raining out?"

"It's been tipping down all night. It started yesterday afternoon." He pauses, then says, "You were lucky. That cave floods in heavy rain."

I think of the slimy trickle of the stream swollen by floodwater and tearing through the cave. I think of the noise of the water filling the cave so you can't hear anything else. I wouldn't have got out. I'd never have climbed back up on my own.

Or would I? I don't know. People do things they'd never believe they could do, if they're desperate enough.

Robert breaks through my thoughts.

"I had to tell your dad," he says abruptly.

"What do you mean?"

"I had to tell him where you'd gone. I know I promised you I wouldn't, but I had to. I had a bad feeling about it. I kept looking at my watch all morning. I knew I should have gone with you."

"I don't think Caz would've taken both of us."

"No. I don't suppose he would. But at least I'd've known more, what he was after."

I move around in the bed, trying to find a comfortable way to lie.

"I don't think he knew," I say slowly. "So how could you have done?"

Robert goes on. "I was mucking out Sheba for Dot because Caz wasn't around. I was just fetching the hay, and suddenly I knew I should never have let you go. I could have done something to stop it. I knew something must've happened. So I shouted to Dot that she'd have to take over and I must've run all the way to your chalet. I don't know what Dot thought. I've never done anything like that before."

He grins. I can see Dot with a bale of hay thrust into her arms, bellowing after Robert. I smile too, and it feels odd because it's the first time I've felt like smiling.

"Your dad didn't say much when I told him. He just said, '*If anything's happened, I'll kill the bastard.*' "

"Did he? That doesn't sound like Dad."

"He was mad. He was really mad. We shot off in your car down to where Caz's dad works. He was there, which is a miracle in itself. Your dad wouldn't let me come in with him, he made me wait outside. You know Caz's dad's a big bloke, but he's all gone to fat with drinking, and your dad was so angry Caz's dad was just backing off. It was funny in a way, from where I was watching. Then the boss came up. He must have been asking if there was any aggravation, and they both went really polite, then the boss disappeared and it all started again. Then your dad came out. He didn't know much more about where Caz was gone, but he said at least Caz was sure of a welcome when he got back. It was half-past-twelve, so we drove back to the chalet in case you'd come back. But you didn't come."

"When did you phone the Cave Rescue people? How did you know which caves we'd gone to?"

Robert looks at me as if my brain's not working.

"We didn't know. How could we? There's hundred of caves on Mendip. Your dad phoned the Cave Rescue to ask their advice, but they said if you'd gone with an experienced caver, you should be OK, and only to let them know if you didn't come back at the time you'd said. What else could they say? You could have been anywhere on Mendip. You never told me where you were going."

"Caz didn't tell me."

"I should have asked you. I should have made you ask him."

"So Caz must have phoned them," I say. A wave of relief washes through me. Caz phoned them. He didn't leave me there, to be found by luck by some party of youth clubbers. Tourists. I wonder why I never thought that it might have been Caz who phoned the Cave Rescue people.

"Yes, he must've," says Robert.

"What do you mean? Didn't you ask him about it?"

"Caz hasn't come back."

"Hasn't come back! But that was yesterday. Where is he?"

"I don't know. Did he say anything to you? Did he say where he was going?"

I try to think. My headache's come back, and the light's hurting my eyes again. I can't get my thoughts together and Robert's looking at me as if he blames me, too, as well as Caz.

"I think he said . . . Yes, he said something about being gone a long time."

I can hear the words now: *That'll keep you warm. In case I'm gone a long time.*

"Well, he has been. No-one's seen him," says Robert. "The van's gone, too, so he could be anywhere."

I think back again. Did Caz say anything else? But I can only remember the little sound of stones hitting rock, and then silence.

"How was he," asks Robert, not looking at my face, "when you were in the cave?"

I don't know what to answer. I feel as if what happened in the cave is between Caz and me. You can't bring it out into the daylight. It belongs there in the dark and the quiet.

"He was upset," I say, and my face twists up and I start to cry.

Robert says nothing. He doesn't try to touch me. He sits there while I cry, and I don't know whether I'm crying because of the way my whole body aches and burns, or because my mum has come down from London, or because Caz did call the Cave Rescue, even though he looked as if he'd forgotten who I was and where we were, or in the end because Caz's mother died years ago, just as Caz had begun to believe that she was going to live.

Chapter Eighteen

I T DIDN'T LEAD to anything, Mum and Dad sharing the chalet while I was in hospital. Things like that don't work out in real life, not when people have been apart for years and years. And I knew that, of course. But it saved Mum a lot of money in bed-and-breakfast, which was a good thing. And I think they did talk quite a bit, mostly about me, because Dad seems to know a lot of things about me now which he didn't know before. And I'm not sure whether that's a good thing or not.

Robert's been round every day. I don't know whether he still blames me or not. We don't talk about Caz, or the cave, or any of what happened. We haven't talked about it since that first morning in hospital. I've talked to Kathy, though. I think she understands Caz better than most people do, even though she didn't like him.

We're staying on here longer than we meant to. I spend most of the time lying down, watching the sun start off at one side of the window and move right over to the other. Or Dad puts a mattress on the grass, and I lie out there. I look up at the sky and the aeroplane trails way up high, and the seagulls, and the clouds moving. I think about Anne Frank watching the leaves come out on the trees under her window. They were horse-chestnuts. I know that, because she wrote about them. Maybe every Spring she thought, *Surely, by next Spring, I'll be out walking under those trees.*

Diane and Paula have gone home. We didn't see so much of them after Mum came down and stayed at the chalet.

Luckily there was no problem about us renting the chalet for an extra week. Edna Tench was delighted. It can't be quite so easy to cram six people into the chalet as she makes out. Bookings are down, with so many people going abroad. And she'd read about me in the papers, so we were quite celebrities, weren't we. She'd cut it out for her scrap-book. There was a column about it in the local paper. *They must be short of news*, Dad said. There was nothing about Caz, just CLOSE SHAVE FOR CAVER, and lots of praise for the Cave Rescue people.

No-one knows anything about Caz. I don't think Caz's dad has told the police about the van. He's not the sort of man who'd go near the police by choice, and there'd be too many questions. So I expect Caz is still driving it. Or he might have dumped it. It would be too risky to try and get the papers to take it abroad. His dad's hoping to hear from Caz through one of these services where people who've left home can leave messages for their families. It's all anonymous. Caz's dad says he'll turn up. I can see he doesn't believe anything bad could really happen to Caz.

Yes, I've met Caz's dad. He's the bloke with the big backside and the sloppy jeans Caz was talking to outside the village shop that morning we went to the cave. He came into hospital to see me. It was embarrassing, because he brought some roses, and I think he'd been drinking at lunchtime. One of the nurses stuck around. I expect she could smell the drink, too. But he wasn't horrible, just sad. He didn't seem to blame me, not even a bit, secretly, like Robert does. I was glad when he went. He doesn't look at all like Caz. But all the same, he's his dad. He looks hopeless, somehow. He kept telling me Caz was a good boy really, just wild.

I dream about Caz most nights. They're not frightening dreams. I just see his eyes, looking down at me, and his mouth is moving, and he's trying to say something. But I can't hear it, although I have the feeling that if I tried, I should be able to hear it. Then he gives that funny little smile, so quick you don't know whether you really saw it or not, and he gets up and walks away. Sometimes he doesn't get up. He smiles, and he's there, then he seems to melt into the darkness and I can't see him any more. It happens over and over. I wake up, but I'm not crying or shaking the way I do after one of my bad dreams. I don't rush to switch on the light. I just lie there in the dark and think about all of it.

I don't know where Caz has gone, but I feel sure somehow that he's gone a long way. He's travelling, which is something he's done all his life, but this time he's on his own and he'll keep on going, as far as he can. I can't believe that there's much here to bring him back. I hope he's OK. I hope he's left something behind in that cave too, something that's been burning away inside him since he was a little kid. Or maybe it's too late for that, and the burning is just part of him now, and it always will be.

As much part of him as being the best-looking person I have ever seen in my life.

While I was in hospital, I told Dad I had to talk to Angelina, and he gave me enough change for a long call.

They brought the phone trolley round to my bed. I told Angelina what had been going on, all of it, even the bits I don't understand any more, the bits I'm tired with trying to understand. Angelina didn't say a lot back, but I knew she was listening, and I knew she'd think it all over, putting her mind to it the way she does. I said I'd see her soon, and I told her how much I'd missed her, how much I wanted to see her. It was the pain in my back, making me want to cry again.

"Hey, Colette, I'll be glad to see *you*! I see you need my eye on you girl!"

She said it like her Aunt Clarisse. Aunt Clarisse used to say that to us, a threat or a promise, when we were kids and misbehaved round at her house. I held on tight to the receiver and the money ticked away second by second.

It's not just where you go, it's the people you meet.

Caz. Caz.

Could do anything, but he won't let himself.

Caz has always wanted to travel.

He takes a bit of getting to know, does Caz.

"*That's Caz talking*," Kathy said.

Mum and I won't be going camping this year. She'll take the time off, but we'll spend it at home. Mum'll have friends round, and I'll go out with Si and Angelina and Josine and Matt. We'll spend all day up at the pool. It'll be late August by the time I get back to London. The days aren't so long any more, and the shops will be full of BACK TO SCHOOL posters, and cheap offers in stationery departments. Enough biros to write THE COMPLETE WORKS OF SHAKESPEARE for £2.99.

I think of the travel-writing prize.

I can't write about old men who invited me in to their tiny whitewashed cottages to eat goat's cheese and figs, and drink wine they'd made from their own grapes. Nor can I write about staring into the mysterious eyes of the Sphinx and wondering what they are trying to express. They aren't real eyes, of course. Just hollows. They're dark because they're empty.

Who would want to read about a journey that ends on the wet, cold floor of a cave underground? Who'd want to read about falling in love and accidents and death and Caz's eyes? Is that going to win any prizes?

I don't think so. It's definitely not a good subject for a school essay.

I could have been in Egypt, or Greece, or Saudi. But I wasn't.

All the same, I'm going to write something.

Also available in **DEFiniTiONS**

THE LEAP

BY

JONATHAN STROUD

He fell without a sound, and the waters of the mill pool closed over him. I sprang to my feet with a cry and leaned out over the edge, scanning the surface. No bubbles rose. There was one swirl of a wave, just one, and then the surface was still again, as calm as ever.

No one believes Charlie when she tells them what happened to Max at the Mill Pool. The doctors and her mother think she is in shock; even her sympathetic brother James cannot begin to understand.

So as she recovers in the hospital bed, Charlie vows to hunt for Max alone. She knows that Max is out there somewhere. And to catch up with him, she'll follow his trail wherever it goes – even beyond the limits of this world. And she'll never give up, no matter what the cost.

ISBN 0099402858   £4.99

Also by Jonathan Stroud:
Buried Fire ISBN 0099402475   £3.99

DEFINITIONS NO MAN'S LAND n. contested land between opposing for

aidan
chambers

POSTCARDS FROM
NO MAN'S LAND

In a richly layered novel, spanning fifty years, Aidan Chambers powerfully evokes the atmosphere of war while brilliantly inter-weaving Jacob's exploration of new relationships in contemporary Amsterdam.

Jacob Todd, abroad on his own for the first time, arrives in Amsterdam for the commemoration of the Battle of Arnhem, where his grandfather fought fifty years before. There, Geertrui Wesseling, now a terminally ill old lady, tells an extraordinary story of love and betrayal which links Jacob with her own Dutch family in a way he never suspected and which leads him to question his place in the world.

'*A superbly crafted, intensely moving novel*' SUNDAY TELEGRAPH
'*Emotive and thought-provoking*' THE BOOKSELLER
'*...the type of serious teenage fiction that should be cherished*' THE INDEPENDENT
'*Writing and literature at its best*' SCHOOL LIBRARIAN
'*Remarkable for ... clear-eyed self-reflection that also characterises* **The Diary of Anne Frank** *and the Rembrandt portraits which Jacob so admires*' TES
'*A terrific novel*' DAILY TELEGRAPH

Winner of the 1999 Carnegie medal
Winner of the 1999 Stockport Book Award

ISBN 0099408627   £5.99

RUNNING out of TIME

BY

Margaret Haddix

'I may have to ask you to do something very dangerous,' Ma said.
Jessie felt a chill. 'What?'
Ma shook her head impatiently. 'You can't ask questions now.'

It's 1840, and in the small village of Clifton the children are dying from an outbreak of diphtheria. There's no medicine to save them and unless help comes soon, a whole generation will be wiped out. Jessie's mother knows how to cure them but it will mean revealing to Jessie the dark and dangerous secret, which lies behind Clifton and its people.

Is Jessie ready to hear the truth? Will she risk her own life to save the lives of the people she loves? And is she prepared for the consequences of running out of time?

ISBN 0099402831   £4.99